IMPRINT OF VIOLENCE . . .

Bert Kling would always remember seeing first the bloody prints, one on each side of the glass-paneled doors. And then the doors swinging open and the girl spilling into the room. Arms wide, hands imploring . . . blue dress torn open over white blood-smeared bra, she lurched toward the muster desk, beseeching Kling to help, for God's sake, help. . . .

BLOOD RELATIVES

BLOOD RELATIVES

by Ed McBain

NAL BOOKS ARE AVAILABLE AT QUANTITY DISCOUNTS WHEN USED TO PROMOTE PRODUCTS OR SERVICES. FOR INFORMATION PLEASE WRITE TO PREMIUM MARKETING DIVISION, THE NEW AMERICAN LIBRARY, INC., 1633 BROADWAY, NEW YORK, NEW YORK 10019.

Published by arrangement with Random House, Inc.

SIGNET TRADEMARK REG. U.S. PAT. OFF. AND FOREIGN COUNTRIES
REGISTERED TRADEMARK—MARCA REGISTRADA
HECHO EN CHICAGO, U.S.A.

SIGNET, SIGNET CLASSICS, MENTOR, PLUME, MERIDIAN AND NAL BOOKS are published by The New American Library, Inc.,
1633 Broadway, New York, New York 10019

First Signet Printing, August, 1982

1 2 3 4 5 6 7 8 9

PRINTED IN THE UNITED STATES OF AMERICA

This is for
Jeff and Anita Ash

The city in these pages is imaginary.
The people, the places are all fictitious.
Only the police routine is based on
established investigatory techniques.

Blood Relatives

One

She came running through the rain shoeless, neon signs and traffic signals splintering in liquid reflection beneath her flying feet. She fled like misjoined Siamese twins, feet touching mirrored feet on the slick black asphalt, puddles of red and green, orange and blue splashing up tintlessly to stain her legs with the gutter filth of the city.

She was bleeding.

She was bleeding from a gash on her right cheek, and she was bleeding from cuts on the palms and fingers of both hands. The front of her dress had been ripped, and she tried to hold the torn sides of the V closed over her brassiere as she ran through the rain. It had been raining since ten o'clock. The rain was neither cruel nor driving now; it had changed to a gentle drizzle that sent mist drifting up from the pavement. In the distance, the green globes of the 87th Precinct shone through the rain and through the mist.

The girl slipped, her feet skidded out from under her. There was a bone-jarring wrench as her hip collided with the pavement. She expelled her breath in pain, and then sat quite still on the sidewalk, her head bent, the rain gently pattering around her. There was blood on her slip, and on her brassiere, smears of blood on her nylon pantyhose. Blood seeped from the open wound on her cheek, blood flamed in the horizontal slashes that crossed her palms and fingers. A traffic light turned to red, suffusing her with color so intense that—for a moment only—it seemed the steady ooze of blood had entirely engulfed the girl. The light clicked into the emptiness of the street. The girl's face, her dress, the cones of her brassiere, the rain-spattered pantyhose, the seething cuts on her hands, the gash on her cheek, all turned green. She struggled to her feet and began running toward the station house.

Detective Bert Kling was at the muster desk, booking a young man who spoke only Spanish. He had just pointed to the Spanish-language version of the warning-of-rights poster. The young man looked up at the sign, nodded, and was beginning to read it silently when the girl burst into the muster room. There were two glass-paneled inner doors behind the wooden doors at the front of the station house. The girl hit those doors with the palms of both hands. Kling heard the thud of her hands hitting the glass panels, and turned immediately. Bloody palmprints. He would always remember seeing first the bloody prints, one on each of the glass-paneled doors. And then the doors swinging open and the girl spilling into the room. Arms wide, hands imploring, cuts on the fingers and palms, open wound on the cheek, wet black hair hanging limply about a pale mascara-streaked face, blue dress torn open over white blood-smeared bra, she lurched toward the muster desk, beseeching Kling to help, for God's sake, help.

* * *

Patrolman Shanahan had wet feet.

The rain had stopped some ten minutes ago, but he'd been sloshing around in it all day now (or at least since three forty-five this afternoon, when he'd relieved Donleavy on post), and his feet were wet and he was developing a chill, and he'd probably be home in bed for a week with the miseries. He was a large man, Shanahan, looking even bigger in the black raingear that billowed out from his massive shoulders like Batman's cape, or maybe Count Dracula's. He carried a nightstick in his right hand, and a flashlight in the other, and he walked along the deserted pavements of this section of his beat, thankful that the rain had stopped, and thankful that it was already eleven-thirty, which meant he'd be relieved in fifteen minutes or so, but not too thankful for the wet feet or the squishy shoes.

He was surprised to see the hand.

The hand lay just outside the open doorway of an abandoned tenement. He could not see an arm attached to the hand, could not in fact see anything beyond the hand and the wrist, and he thought for a frightening moment that the hand had been severed from the rest of the body. But then he saw the faint outline of an arm, and beyond that, the shape of a body lying just inside and athwart the entrance to the building. He went up the wide flat steps of the front stoop to where the hand lay palm up on the top step, and he flashed his light onto the curled fingers and saw the cuts on the palm and the fingers and the wrist, and knew before he threw his light into the hallway that this was going to be a bad one.

He realized with a start that he was standing in blood, and recoiled from it in horror, as though it were capable of dissolving the soles of his shoes. As he backed away from the sticky puddle underfoot, the beam of his torch swung slightly higher, and he saw the body now and felt immediately sick to his stomach. He looked over his shoulder quickly, perhaps because death was so suddenly palpable in that narrow cubicle, perhaps because he was embarrassed by his reaction and wanted to make certain no one had seen it. The girl lay on her back in the blood. She was perhaps sixteen years old, and she had dark hair, and brown eyes that were open wide and staring up at the ceiling overhead. The ceiling was bloated with water that seemed ready to burst through the plaster and inundate the small entryway. The girl was wearing a pink dress that had been slashed to tatters. The knife had been relentless, cutting through fabric and flesh indiscriminately, gashes crossing and criss-crossing, overlapping in frenzy and fury, open angry trenches on her breasts and on her face— Shanahan turned away and vomited into his hand when he realized the girl's nose was hanging from her face by a single sliver of skin.

Then he went to the box on the corner and called the precinct.

Monoghan without Monroe was like bagels without lox—Carella hardly recognized the man without his partner. In this city, the detective catching a homicide was responsible for the case from that moment on, but the Homicide Division nonetheless sent an obligatory team of detectives to the scene, presumably to lend their expertise to the investigation, or perhaps to guarantee a dignity appropriate to the seriousness of the crime. Monoghan and Monroe worked as a team out of Homicide, but tonight there was only Monoghan, and he sounded like a voice without an echo, looked like a body without a shadow. His partner was sick, he explained. The flu. More damn flu around this month. Wearing a black overcoat, white handkerchief in the breast pocket, black snap-brim fedora, black leather gloves, white silk muffler, black bowtie behind it, Monoghan seemed dressed for the Governor's Ball, or at least the opera. He told Carella at once that he had been dragged away from an anniversary party, a *golden* anniversary no less, and hoped he could get back to it before long. He seemed to imply that Carella had personally caused the death of the young girl who lay in the hallway in her own blood.

"How old you suppose she is?" Monoghan asked. "Her age, I mean," he added immediately, as though sorely missing Monroe and trying to supply in monologue the endlessly redundant dialogue that had become their trademark over the years.

"She looks sixteen or seventeen," Carella said.

He was staring at the open wounds all over the girl's body. He could never get used to it, *would* never get used to this senseless reduction of flesh to rubble. Ten minutes ago, a half-hour ago, the girl had been alive. She now lay in angular disarray in an alien hallway, her life juices spilled around her as carelessly as dirty water from a dish basin. He looked at her corpse and squinched his eyes in pain, and when Monoghan commented that the guy had probably raped her first, since her pantyhose were all ripped and bloody around the crotch, Carella said nothing.

In a little while the assistant medical examiner arrived. Like any other physician called out on a rainy night, he was grumpy. The fact that this was a Saturday, when people were supposed to be out having a good time instead of examining homicide victims, did little to enliven his spirits. "No rest for the weary," he said, and put his black bag down beside the dead girl.

"Well, at least the rain's stopped," Monoghan said.

"You know what they do in England when it rains, don't you?" the M.E. asked.

"No, what?"

"They let it rain," the M.E. said, and both men burst out laughing.

"Rain brings out the bedbugs," Monoghan said. "Had to be a bedbug did something like this."

"A lunatic," the M.E. said.

"A crazy person," Monoghan said, and smiled. He had found a substitute for Monroe. Even on this damp Saturday night, criminal detection could proceed in an orderly Tweedledum and Tweedledee fashion. His mood perceptibly brightened. "Did a nice job on her," he said conversationally.

"Yep. Cut the trachea, the carotid, and the jugular," the M.E. said.

"Notice her hands?" Monoghan said.

"Getting to them," the M.E. said.

To Carella, apparently feeling amplification was necessary, Monoghan said, "In some of these incised wound homicides, you get these defense cuts. Person puts up his arm to block the knife, he'll get cut on the fingers someplace."

"Or the wrist," the M.E. said.

"Or the forearm."

"Or the palm."

"I hate knife wounds, don't you?" Monoghan said. "You get a bullet wound, it's neat. Knife wounds are messy."

"I've seen messy bullet wounds, too," the M.E. said.

"But not as messy as knife wounds. I hate knife wounds."

"I hate blunt-force wounds," the M.E. said. "But your bullet wounds can get pretty messy, too."

"I'm not talking about your shotgun wounds now," Monoghan said.

"No, I'm talking about your average exit wound from a .45-caliber slug, for example. Drive a subway train through that exit wound. That's a messy wound."

"Still, I hate knife wounds worse than anything else."

"Well, to each his own," the M.E. said, and shrugged, and snapped his bag shut. "She's all yours," he said, and rose from where he'd been crouching over the girl.

"Was she raped?" Monoghan asked.

"Can't tell you that till we get her downtown," the M.E. said.

In the girl's handbag, they found a comb, a package of menthol cigarettes, a book of matches, three dollars and forty cents in cash, and a Social Security card that told them her name was Muriel Stark.

At twenty minutes past midnight a woman named Lillian Lowery called the precinct and asked to talk to a detective. When Sergeant Murchison asked what it was in reference to, she told him she was worried about her daughter and her niece, who had gone to a party at eight o'clock and who were not yet home. Murchison asked her to hold, and then put her through to Detective Meyer Meyer upstairs in the squadroom.

The woman immediately told Meyer that the girls were only fifteen and seventeen years old respectively, and that they had promised to be home by eleven o'clock at the very latest. When they had not arrived by eleven-thirty, she had called the house where the party was still going on, and a boy who answered the phone told her they'd left at least an hour before that. It should have taken them no more than twenty minutes to get home. It was now almost twelve-thirty—which meant that nearly two hours had elapsed since they'd left the party. Meyer, who had a daughter himself, gently suggested to Mrs. Lowery that perhaps *her* daughter and niece had decided to take a walk with some of the boys who'd been at the party, but Mrs. Lowery insisted her daughter was very good about keeping her word; if, for example, she knew she was going to be late, she always called home to say so. Which is why Mrs. Lowery was worried. Meyer took down a description of the girls, and then asked for their full names. Mrs. Lowery said her daughter's name was Patricia Lowery, and her niece's name was Muriel Stark.

Meyer asked her to call him again if the girls showed up; if he did not hear from her by morning, he would pass the information on to the Missing Persons Bureau. In the meantime, he phoned down to the desk sergeant and asked him to put out a 10-69 to all the precinct's radio motor patrol cars, specifying a non-crime alert for two dark-haired, brown-eyed, teenage girls, one wearing a blue, the other a pink dress, last seen in the vicinity of 1214 Harding, and presumably heading south toward their home at 648 St. John's Road. Meyer gave the desk sergeant the girls' names, of course, but neither of those names meant anything to him. He had come on duty shortly before midnight, and did not know that both Kling and Carella were actively investigating two separate cases involving two teenage girls. His ignorance wasn't particularly uncommon; no one expected every detective on the squad to know what every other detective on the squad was doing at any given hour of the day. Kling, for example, did not know that Carella was at this moment in the hospital mortuary waiting for a necropsy report that would tell him whether or not Muriel Stark had been raped. And Carella did not know that Kling was on the eighth floor of that same hospital talking to an intern who said it would now be all right for him to interrogate the girl who had burst into the muster room two hours earlier. Kling hadn't even known her name until the intern gave it to him.

At 12:33 A.M. Patricia Lowery put some of the pieces together for them.

The first thing she told Kling was that her cousin Muriel had been killed. She told Kling where the slaying had taken place, and Kling went immediately to the telephone at the nurse's station in the corridor outside and called the precinct—only to learn that Carella had responded to the homicide an hour ago. The desk sergeant checked the log, in fact, and told Kling that Carella was at that moment in the hospital mortuary. Kling thanked him, and before going back into Patricia's room, called down to the mortuary to tell Carella where he was and to advise him that he was about to interrogate an eyewitness to the crime. Carella told him to hold off for a minute, he'd be right upstairs.

They had washed her and dressed her wounds and given her a clean hospital gown. Her hair was neatly combed and her eyes were dry. A police stenographer sat by the bed, his pencil poised over his pad, ready to record every word. Carella and Kling asked their questions softly. Patricia answered in a clear, steady voice, recalling emotionlessly and without horror the events that had taken place after she and her cousin left the party.

CARELLA: That was at what time?
PATRICIA: We left at about ten-thirty.
KLING: Were you heading home?
PATRICIA: Yes.
KLING: Can you tell us what happened?
PATRICIA: It began raining again. It was raining on and off all night. It slowed down when we left, and then it began again. So we were running down the street, ducking in doorways and under awnings, like that. We weren't wearing raincoats because when we went to the party it wasn't raining. We were maybe two blocks from Paul's house when it started raining.
CARELLA: Paul?
PATRICIA: Paul Gaddis. He's the boy who had the party. It was his birthday. His eighteenth birthday.
CARELLA: How old are you, Patricia?
PATRICIA: Fifteen. I'll be sixteen in December. December the twelfth.
CARELLA: And your cousin was how old?
PATRICIA: Seventeen.
CARELLA: All right, go ahead. You were walking from Paul's house . . .
PATRICIA: Yes.
KLING: On Harding was this?
PATRICIA: Yes. Where all the stores are. Near Harding and Sixteenth. It was raining very hard when we got to Sixteenth, so we stopped under an awning for a while, until it let up. Then we started walking down Harding again, toward Fourteenth. There's construction going on around there, these buildings are being knocked down, they're putting up a housing project. So when we got to Fourteenth, it began raining again, and Muriel and I ran into the hallway of this aban-

doned building. Just to get out of the rain. Till it let up a little. We were only three or four blocks from where we lived, we figured we'd wait a few minutes and then go home.

KLING: Did your cousin live with you, is that it?

PATRICIA: Yes. She came to live with us when I was thirteen. Her parents got killed in an automobile accident on the turnpike.

CARELLA: Do you have any brothers or sisters, Patricia?

PATRICIA: Yes, I have an older brother.

CARELLA: What's his name?

PATRICIA: Andrew Lowery.

CARELLA: How old is he?

PATRICIA: Nineteen.

CARELLA: Does he still live at home?

PATRICIA: Yes.

CARELLA: Was he at the party tonight?

PATRICIA: No, he was working.

KLING: What kind of work does he do?

PATRICIA: Well, it's only part-time. There's this steak joint on the Stem, they call him when they need help, usually on a Saturday night. I guess if he hadn't been working, he'd have come to the party with us. And then what happened wouldn't have happened.

KLING: Do you want to tell us what happened now?

PATRICIA: Yes. We were standing in the hallway there, looking out at the rain. I didn't think it would ever let up. I kept telling Muriel we should just make a run for it, you know, but she didn't want to ruin her dress. It was coming down in sheets by then, I guess she was right. Still . . .

KLING: What time was this?

PATRICIA: It must've been close to eleven.

CARELLA: Go on.

PATRICIA: There was nobody on the street, everything was deserted because it was raining so hard. We must've stood in the hallway there for at least five minutes without even seeing a car go by. Then—I still don't know how he got there, he must've been in the building all along, maybe sleeping in one of the empty apartments or something—this man was suddenly there. He just stepped out of the shadows behind us, and he grabbed Muriel by the wrist, and she screamed, or at least she started to scream. But then she saw he had a knife and she shut up even before he told her to shut up. I guess *my* first reaction was to run, to get away from there. But he was holding the knife on Muriel, and I figured if I did anything like that, he might hurt her just out of spite. So I stood there. I guess you just figure, in a situation like that, that it isn't going to get worse, it's just going to work out someway, somebody'll come to save you.

CARELLA: Did you recognize this man? Was he anyone you knew, or anyone you'd seen before?

PATRICIA: No. He was a perfect stranger.

CARELLA: Can you describe him to us?

PATRICIA: Yes. He was a tall man. About as tall as you, I would say. Six-two, or six-three.

CARELLA: That would make him taller than I am.

PATRICIA: Well, no, he was about your height. A little huskier, though.

CARELLA: Was he white or black?

PATRICIA: White.

CARELLA: Did you notice what color his hair was?

PATRICIA: Dark. Either brown or black, but very dark.

KLING: And his eyes?

PATRICIA: He had blue eyes.

KLING: Was he clean-shaven, or did he have a mustache or beard?

PATRICIA: Clean-shaven.

CARELLA: What was he wearing?

PATRICIA: A suit, I think. Or else slacks and a sports jacket, I'm not sure. If it was a sports jacket, it was a solid color. And dark.

CARELLA: Shirt and tie?

PATRICIA: No tie.

CARELLA: Would you recognize him if you saw him again?

PATRICIA: Yes. There wasn't any light in the hallway, but there was light from the streetlamp. I'd recognize him. And I'd also recognize his voice.

KLING: You said he told your cousin to shut up . . .

PATRICIA: Yes, that was after she'd stopped screaming already. She screamed when he first came out of the darkness, and then she saw the knife and stopped screaming, but he told her to shut up, anyway.

KLING: What else did he say?

PATRICIA: That he wouldn't hurt us if we did what he told us to do. He was holding Muriel by the wrist, and I was sort of against the opposite wall. He had the knife pointed at Muriel.

CARELLA: What kind of knife was it?

PATRICIA: What do you mean?

CARELLA: A switchblade or . . . ?

PATRICIA: No, no, it was a regular knife. Like the kind of knife you see in a kitchen.

CARELLA: A long knife, or a short one?

PATRICIA: I guess the blade was about four inches long.

CARELLA: And when he came out of the darkness, he had the knife in his hand already?

PATRICIA: Yes.

CARELLA: From which direction did he come? The right of the entrance hall, or the left?

PATRICIA: The right, I think. Yes. Muriel was standing on the right, so that's where he must have come from. Because it was Muriel he grabbed, you see.

KLING: What happened after he told Muriel to shut up?

PATRICIA: He made her get down on her knees in front of him. And then he told her she was going to do what he wanted her to do. He said go on, take it, I know you want it. I was watching them. I was standing against the wall, watching them. I thought after she did it, I thought that would be the end of it. But he suddenly started stabbing her, he was . . . it was terrible to watch, he just stabbed her again and again and I stood there watching what he was doing to her and I couldn't believe this was happening, I couldn't believe he was *doing* this to her, I almost couldn't believe my own eyes. And I knew what would happen next, I knew he would force *me* to do the same thing, first promising he wouldn't hurt me, but hurting me afterwards, anyway. I realized I had to run, but somehow I couldn't move, I just watched while he kept doing it to her. And then he . . .

CARELLA: Patricia, you don't need to . . .

PATRICIA: I *want* to tell you, I want to tell you everything. He turned to me, and he said You're next, and I thought he meant he was going to force me the way he'd forced Muriel, but then I realized he was going to kill me, he was coming at me with the knife, he was moving the knife toward my face. I put out my hand to protect myself, I threw back my arm, you know, like this, to try to protect my face, and he cut me across the palm of my hand, I guess it was, and I threw up my other hand, and he kept forcing me back against the wall and slashing at my hands. He ripped open the front of my dress with the tip of the knife, and I remembered what he had done to Muriel's breasts, and I began screaming at the top of my lungs, but no one heard me, there was nobody in the neighborhood, it's a construction site, you see. That was when he cut me on the cheek, when I was screaming, here under the eye. I don't know how I got away from him, I think I must have kicked him. I remember he was groaning on the floor when I ran out of the building, so I guess I must have kicked him. Then I heard him yelling behind me, and I heard him coming down the steps after me, and I knew if he caught me he would kill me the way he'd killed Muriel. I was thinking ahead by then. I was thinking if I ran home, he could catch me going up the stairs, we live on the third floor, he could catch me in the hallway. But if I ran to the police station, if I could just get to the police station, then there'd be cops all around, and he wouldn't be able to hurt me. So that's where I ran, to the police station.

KLING: Was he following you?

PATRICIA: I don't know. I think so. But I slipped and fell when I was about two blocks from the station house, and I didn't hear anybody behind me, so maybe he'd given up by then. Will you catch him?

In the mortuary downstairs, the coroner gave Carella and Kling a verbal necropsy report on Muriel Stark. Though she had suffered many wounds during the brutal assault, the coroner told them that the fatal wound had most likely been a gaping incision of the left shoulder and neck, six and one-half inches long, and one and one-quarter inches deep, which had completely severed the left common carotid artery and internal jugular vein, and extended through the left lobe of the thyroid and anterior portion of the trachea. Death, in the coroner's opinion, had probably resulted from external hemorrhage, attended by inhalation of infused blood, and supervening pulmonary air embolism.

The coroner explained that in most homicides where rape was suspected, the examiner searched for injuries of the genital organs, blood and semen stains, and foreign hairs or other foreign substances. The coroner had found no traces of seminal fluid in the dead girl's vaginal, rectal, or digestive tracts, and there had been no semen stains on her clothing. This did not eliminate the possibility of rape; it merely indicated that there had been no attendant ejaculation. Neither did he find foreign hairs or substances, but there was one wound that indicated the crime might have been sexually motivated, a wound which in itself had hemorrhaged severely enough to have been a possible cause of death. This wound had been the result of the tearing of the vaginal vault, the introduction into the pelvis of a sharp instrument, most probably the murder weapon, and the subsequent tearing of the left common iliac artery. At this point the coroner asked if he might introduce an opinion somewhat beyond the scope of pathology or toxicology, and then suggested to the detectives that perhaps they were dealing with a sadistic killer here, the murder having all the earmarks of so-called "lust" murders, in which the perpetrator's libido could be satisfied only by slaying. The coroner mentioned again that he was not a psychiatrist, of course, and this was merely his opinion.

The detectives thanked him, and then went uptown again to the abandoned tenement on Fourteenth and Harding.

Two

The homicide was officially Carella's, and as the detective in charge of the investigation, he had promptly notified the desk officer and asked him to make the necessary calls that were the routine aftermath of any murder. The desk sergeant had immediately notified the office of the chief medical examiner, and then had called the Communications Unit to give them the aided number and the M.E.'s report number. He had then informed Detective-Lieutenant Byrnes, who commanded the 87th Squad, and Captain Frick, who commanded the entire precinct, that a homicide investigation was in progress. And then he had called the Chief of Detectives' office, and the Section Command and District Office, and the Homicide Division, and the Photo Unit, and the Police Lab, and the Latent Unit, and he would have called Ballistics had a gun been involved in the murder, and he was ready to call the D.A.'s office with a request for an attorney and a stenographer should the perpetrator be apprehended, as they say in the trade. (He also called his wife to tell her things had begun jumping and he might be home late.)

At the scene earlier, Carella had instructed the man from the Photo Unit to take his Polaroids of the dead girl and the murder scene so that Carella could put a U.F.95 tag on her toe and get her to the hospital for immediate autopsy. There was no electricity in the abandoned building, so Carella ordered floodlights from the Emergency Service Division, and these were in place and operating by the time the ambulance came to pick up the murdered girl's body. By then, too, the area had been roped off and posted with CRIME SCENE and NO SMOKING signs. The signs warning against smoking had nothing to do with cancer. Cigars or cigarettes were often valuable evidence, and the investigating officer didn't want a bunch of *good* guys dropping their butts in with something the *bad* guy may have left behind.

Carella had drawn his own pencil sketch of the crime scene, and then—together with the lab technician—had begun looking for (a) the murder weapon and (b) any traces of hair, clothing, excrement, urine, or stains that might have been left by the killer before, during, or immediately following the murder. At the same time he instructed the man from Latent to conduct a thorough search for fingerprints and footprints that could be compared against the dead girl's. (There was, at the moment, an imprint of a size-twelve gunboat in the sticky hallway blood—but that was Officer Shanahan's.) When Carella left for the hospital, he did so secure in the knowledge that a team of highly trained professionals was busily at work looking for any evidence that might help identify the murderer. He did not know, of course, until Kling called him in the mortuary, that the murder had been witnessed, or that Patricia Lowery was alive and entirely capable of identifying the killer.

He now tried to retrace, with Kling and the lab technician, the route Patricia must have taken from the tenement to the police station. He did not expect to find any traces of blood on the route; the rain had undoubtedly washed them all away. Nor was he particularly interested in locating either Patricia's shoes or her handbag. She had arrived at the precinct shoeless, and carrying nothing in her bleeding hands; presumably, she had either lost her shoes and handbag in her desperate rush for freedom, or else had deliberately discarded them. Carella was interested only in finding the murder weapon. If the killer had indeed pursued her from that abandoned building, he must have been carrying the weapon during his chase. It was entirely possible he had finally thrown it away somewhere along the route.

They found one of Patricia's high-heeled satin pumps half a block away from the tenement. It was stained only with muddy water. A little way beyond that, they found the second pump. This one had bloodstains near the heel. The three men—Carella, Kling, and the lab technician—debated the meaning of this. They finally decided that the first pump had *fallen* from Patricia's foot, but that she had deliberately taken off the second pump after hobbling along on just one shoe for some ten or fifteen yards. She had undoubtedly grabbed the pump near the heel when removing it, and the bloodstains were probably from her own palm. Three blocks beyond where they'd found the second pump, they found Patricia's handbag. It was a long, narrow bag, some ten inches in length, some four inches wide, covered in blue satin that matched the high-heeled pumps. There were bloodstains on the satin. Inside the bag, they found a package of cigarettes, a lighter, a comb, a change purse with sixty-three cents in it, four loose subway tokens, and a wallet containing seventeen dollars and a photograph of a slender young man with dark hair and dark eyes.

They did not find the knife that had been used to murder Muriel Stark. But five blocks from the tenement in which she had been killed, they found a man sleeping in the doorway of a Chinese laundry. The man was wearing a dark suit and a white shirt, no tie. His hair was brown. There appeared to be bloodstains on the front of his white shirt.

"Hey, wake up," Carella said.

"Go 'way," the man said.

"You," Carella said. "Wake up."

Kling flashed his light onto the man's face. The

man opened his eyes and then immediately closed them against the glare. His eyes were blue, they had seen that. And Patricia Lowery had described the murderer as a dark-haired man with blue eyes.

"What do you want, huh?" he said, and turned his head to one side and squinted his eyes only partially open.

"What are you doing here?" Carella asked.

"Trying to sleep," the man said.

"What's that on your shirt?" Kling asked.

"Where? What do you mean?"

"There. Is that blood?"

"Yeah, that's blood. What do you guys want?"

"We're police officers," Carella said, and flashed his shield.

"Oh, shit," the man said.

"What's your name?"

"Louis Sully."

"How do you spell that?"

"S-u-l-l-y."

"What are you doing here this hour of the night?"

"I told you. Trying to get some sleep."

"How'd you get that blood on your shirt?"

"I was in a fight."

"Where?"

"Bar I go to."

"How long have you been here in this doorway?"

"I don't know. What time is it?"

"It's a little past two."

"I don't know."

"When did you have your fight?"

"Around ten-thirty, eleven o'clock. You got a cigarette? Anybody got a cigarette?"

"Here," the lab technician said, and extended a pack to him.

"Thanks," Sully said, and shook a cigarette free from the pack and then lit it. The detectives watched him silently. He handed the pack back to the lab technician.

"You were in a bar and got into a fight, is that it?" Carella said.

"Yeah, hit a man in the nose," Sully said.

"And he bled all over your shirt, huh?"

"Yeah."

"Anybody see this fight?"

"No, nobody saw it."

"How come? Was the bar empty?"

"No, the bar wasn't empty, but it didn't happen *in* the bar, it happened *outside* the bar."

"Then no one saw the fight."

"That's right, no one saw it. Except the guy I was fighting."

"And who was that?"

"I don't know his name," Sully said.

"You had a fight with a man whose name you don't know."

"That's right. He was in the bar there, and we got into an argument, and he invited me to step outside."

"Anybody hear this argument?"

"I don't know what anybody heard or didn't."

"Anybody see you going outside with him?"

"I don't know."

"What'd you do after the fight?"

"I chased him up the street, and then I went back inside the bar and called my wife. She said I was a drunken bum and I shouldn't bother coming home. So I started looking for a place to sleep."

"What time was this?"

"When I called the wife? I told you. Around ten-thirty, eleven, something like that."

"What'd you do then?"

"I left the bar and I went over my friend's house. Larry. But he wasn't home. So then I stopped at a liquor store and bought a pint, and I found this doorway and sat here drinking till I fell asleep. What is this, anyway? I don't like getting stopped by cops and questioned right in the street."

"Have you ever been questioned by the police before? In the street or anyplace else?"

"Once."

"Why were you questioned?"

"There was a burglary in my building."

"And the police questioned you about it?"

"Yeah."

"Why'd they do that?"

"Well, they questioned everybody about it."

"You've never been *involved* in a burglary, have you?"

"No, no."

"Have you ever been involved in *any* crime?"

"No."

"Mr. Sully, we're going to have to take you with us," Carella said.

"What for?"

"Well, for one thing, we'd like to test those bloodstains on your . . ."

Sully came up out of the doorway in a crouch, flicking the cigarette away with his right hand and then throwing his left fist into Carella's gut, doubling him over. Kling grabbed for Sully, but he shoved past him, knocking him flat to the wet pavement. He was sprinting for the street when the lab technician tackled him. Sully fell headlong to the sidewalk, and then began crawling and kicking toward the curb, the technician hanging onto his legs for dear life. Kling jumped up and onto Sully's back, and then twisted his arms behind him and cuffed his wrists together. Sully kicked out once more at the lab technician, who sat bolt upright on the sidewalk now and blinked into the night. He was surprised and somewhat thrilled by his own behavior; this was the first time he'd ever physically apprehended a criminal. He could not wait to get home to tell his wife about it. Trouble was, she probably wouldn't believe him.

It was three o'clock in the morning. In the squadroom, it was technically Sunday, but it still felt like Saturday. They did not tell Sully that a teenage girl had been murdered five blocks from where they'd found him sleeping in a doorway. They told him only that they were going to book him for assaulting two police officers, and then they said they wanted to ask him a few questions, if that was all right with him. He did not have to answer any questions if he didn't want to.

"Questions about what?" Sully asked.

"About what you were doing in that doorway. And about why you decided to assault . . ."

"I didn't assault anybody," Sully said. "I took a poke at you, and I shoved your partner. That's all I did."

"That's assault," Carella said.

"If that's assault, what is it when you *really* hurt somebody?" Sully said, and shook his head.

"Look, Mr. Sully . . ."

"Anyway, did I hurt you?" Sully asked. "Tell the truth, did I hurt you?"

"No, you didn't hurt me," Carella said.

"Then how about giving me a break, huh? I didn't hurt anybody, so how about letting me out of here, huh? How about forgetting that assault stuff, okay? Who assaulted anybody? All I did was take a feeble little poke at . . ."

"Mr. Sully, would you care to answer some questions, or wouldn't you?" Carella said.

"Sure, I'd care to answer some questions. If that'll help you forget the assault stuff, sure I'll answer . . ."

"I can't make any promises," Carella said.

"I realize that," Sully said, and winked. "What kind of questions have you got?"

"Mr. Sully, the big one is why you resisted arrest back there. We identified ourselves as police officers, you *knew* we were police officers, yet you hit me . . ."

"But I didn't hurt you," Sully said immediately.

"You hit me nonetheless, and you knocked my partner to the sidewalk . . ."

"I only shoved him, he must've slipped," Sully said.

"Why'd you do that, Mr. Sully?"

"Because I'm scared of cops," Sully said.

"You're scared of cops, so you go around slugging them and pushing them . . ."

"No, I panicked, that's all. I didn't want to end up in a police station. I'm scared of cops."

"Is there any reason for that?"

"No reason."

"You're just scared of cops."

"Yeah. That's all. Yeah. It's a phobia."

"Mr. Sully, have you ever been arrested before?"

"Never."

"Mr. Sully, we can't check with the Identification Section till eight in the morning, but at that time we'll find out whether there's a yellow sheet on you . . ."

"No, no, I've never been arrested."

"You're sure about that."

"Positive. I've had complaints made, but I've never been arrested."

"What kind of complaints?"

"Complaints. People make complaints. A person gets a little drunk, people make complaints."

"Which people?"

"Well, a person's wife, for example. A person gets a little drunk, he slaps his wife around a little, right away she calls the cops."

"Has your wife complained to the police about you?"

"Well, just a few times. Three or four times."

"Because you beat her?"

"Well, I wouldn't say I beat her. I just slapped her around a little. You know. Little slapping around. Have a few drinks, slap her around a little. That's all."

"Where'd you get the blood on your shirt, Mr. Sully?"

"Well, you know."

"Was it in a fight outside a bar?"

"Well, not exactly."

"Where was it?"

"Well, in the bedroom."

"Your bedroom?"

"Yeah. That's right. Yes, my bedroom. I had a few drinks, you know, so I went in there and she was brushing her hair, so I told her to stop that. She's sitting there brushing her hair and counting, it can drive a person crazy, somebody sitting there and counting out loud. Fifty, fifty-one, fifty-two, her arm going like a piston, and she's counting, fifty-three, fifty-four, I told her to cut it out. So she didn't cut it out, so I hit her. So she was bleeding a little from the nose, nothing serious. So she told me to get the hell out, which I did. I went over Larry's house, but he wasn't home, so then I bought a pint, and I was in the doorway sleeping. I thought maybe she'd filed another complaint. That's why I tried to get away from you guys. Look, I'll tell you the truth, I don't know how bad I hurt her this time. I was pretty drunk, I hit her hard. She was bleeding a lot when I left the house. So I didn't want any trouble with the law, I mean a man and his wife can work things out between them, am I right? We've always worked things out between us. So okay, I slap her around every now and then, but she knows I love her."

"Uh-huh," Carella said.

"I do."

"Sure."

"So now I told you what you wanted to know, so how about let's forget this assault stuff, okay?"

"I've got a better idea," Carella said.

"Yeah, what's that?"

"How about we send a car over to your house, see how your wife is doing, first of all. Then how about we check those bloodstains on your shirt with your wife's blood, just to make sure it isn't somebody *else's* blood, okay? That'll have to wait till morning, when the lab opens. Meanwhile, just for the fun of it, how about we book you for two counts of assault, okay?"

"*Two* counts? My wife won't press charges against me, she loves me too much."

"We don't."

"Huh?"

"Me. And my partner. One, two. Two counts," Carella said. "And that may be the least of your worries, Mr. Sully. Depending on what the lab has to say about those bloodstains."

The lab got back to them at ten the next morning. It told them that whereas Muriel Stark's blood had been of the O group, and Patricia Lowery's was of the A group; and whereas the scene of the crime and the bodies and clothing of both victims (the dead one *and* the living one) had been liberally sprinkled or spattered or smeared with blood from *both* groups, the stains on Louis Sully's shirt were nonetheless of the B group, which substantiated his story about the fracas with his wife, since *her* blood happened to be in that group too. As for the lady, Sully had fractured not only her nose, but her jaw and her collarbone as well. At about the same time Patricia Lowery was being released from the hospital that morning, Mrs. Louis Sully was being moved from a ward to a semi-private room, which her doting husband had requested for her.

Carella and Kling, in the squadroom of the 87th, went through their file of known sex offenders, and then put out a request for similar files from every other detective squad in the city. It was eleven o'clock on a Sunday morning. Carella went home to his family. Kling went directly to Augusta Blair's apartment.

During World War II, American bomber crews would fly out from bases in England to strike at enemy targets on the continent. They would fly through exploding flak, helpless in the grip of the bombsight, unable to veer from enemy fire, unable to dodge enemy aircraft until the bombs were released and the controls were back again in the hands of the pilot. And in the evening and in the night they would sit and drink in English country pubs, throw darts with the good old boys, sing an American song or two, and try to forget the terror they had known in the skies over Germany.

During the Vietnam war, combat infantrymen were flown to Saigon by helicopter from bases in the boonies, and from Saigon they were jetted to Hawaii or Japan for what was called R&R—Rest & Recuperation. They would go back into the jungle afterwards, presumably refreshed and capable of once more dealing with the everyday horrors of warfare. There existed, for the airmen in World War II, and even for the foot soldiers in the Vietnam war, a curious form of double-think that allowed them to be combat troops one moment and quasi-civilians the next. In the morning you dropped a stick of bombs down a factory smokestack, and in the evening you dropped an egg into your lager. On Friday you were laying machine-gun fire across a trail leading into a suspect hamlet, and on Monday you were laying a whore in Honolulu. Helped you keep your sanity, they said. Moderation in everything, and everything in moderation.

It was something like that for cops.

When it got too horrible, you went home. You took a shower and changed your clothes. You mixed yourself a cold martini or a hot toddy. You patted your dog on the head or your wife on the behind. You philosophized a bit, maybe wagging your head or clucking your tongue every so often. After all (you told yourself), if a person chooses to become a policeman instead of, say, a florist, then he's got to realize he will more often be dealing with violence than with violets. If he chooses to become a cop in the first place, then he's got to recognize in the second place that the cops are a paramilitary organization, and that's because they are involved in a daily war, and that is a war against crime, ta-ra! And in any war, you've got your victims, so if you can't stand the sight of blood, then you shouldn't become either a cop or a noted brain surgeon—who anyway makes a lot more money than a cop does. Or a butcher, either, if you can't stand the sight of blood. But if you *do* become a cop, then there are also certain tricks of the trade you have to learn early if you hope to survive, and one of those tricks is the very same one the bomber crews learned in World War II, and the hapless infantrymen learned in the Vietnamese adventure—how to enjoy being a civilian every now and then. Carella went home to his family, and Kling went to see Augusta Blair.

There were those detectives on the squad who wondered aloud, and *always* in Kling's presence, whether or not he really intended marrying that poor girl. Not that he was worth even her pinkie. A beauty such as Augusta Blair, whose face and form adorned the covers (not to mention the pages) of fashion and service magazines, whose somewhat breathy voice issued from radio and television loudspeakers alike, she of the jade-green eyes and auburn hair, she of the high cheekbones and even white teeth, she of the good breasts, narrow waist, wide hips, and splendid wheels—what right had a clod like Kling even to *consider* expecting her hand in marriage? Which he had expected. And which he'd asked for. And which she'd agreed to give to him. But that had been back in January, when a hood named Randall M. Nesbitt (the *world* might forget what he had done, or almost done, but Kling never would) had caused an upheaval in West Riverhead the likes of which the cops had never before seen, and never *hoped* to see again. Kling had asked Augusta to marry him on the night Nesbitt led his misguided street troops on what was to have been his last glorious peace-keeping mission. She had said yes moments before Kling walked to the phone and heard Carella's voice urging him to get uptown because all hell was breaking loose. That had been in January. This was now September. The boys of the 87th wanted a wedding, or at least a bar mitzvah. But Meyer Meyer's youngest son would not be thirteen till next summer, and Cotton Hawes showed no indication of *ever* asking Christine Maxwell to marry him, so that left Kling and Augusta as the only immediate possibilities on the horizon.

Sanity. It all had to do with keeping one's sanity. Weddings, birthdays, bar mitzvahs, anniversaries (no funerals, thank you; the squad dealt with too *many* funerals, most of them involving dead strangers), whatever joyous occasion the squad could find to celebrate, whatever helped to create a flimsy sense of tradition was all to the good. Like those World War II bomber crews, they were only protecting their sanity. They were finding opportunities that made them feel like ordinary civilians every now and then. They were keeping the old aspidistra flying. It would have gladdened their hearts, those sentimental old bastards, to have known that on this Sunday morning in September—Sunday, September 7, to be exact—Kling and Augusta were discussing plans for their wedding. They were, in fact, trying to decide which members of the squad should be *invited* to the wedding.

"The thing I don't want this to turn into," Augusta said, "is some kind of Patrolmen's Benevolent Association event, if you know what I mean."

"Or a meeting of the Emerald Society," Kling said.

"Or something, you know, that looks like all the cops in the city are gathered to hear the Police Commissioner speak instead of *us* getting married."

"I understand completely," Kling said.

"So please don't get upset," Augusta said.

"I'm not upset," Kling said. "It's just that most of these guys I've worked with a long time, and I've *got* to invite them. I'm not only talking now about the ones I *want* to invite—like Steve or Meyer or Hal or Cotton or the Lieutenant or Bob or . . ."

"Bert, that's half the squad already!"

"No, honey, there are sixteen men on the squad."

"And if you add wives to that . . ."

"Not all of them are married. Gus, I'll tell you the truth, I'd really *like* to invite all of them, I mean it. Because these are guys I work with, you know. So how can I invite *some* of them and not others? I may be on the job, say, with Andy Parker one night, and some hood'll get the drop on me, and Andy'll remember I didn't invite him to my wedding, and he'll forget to shoot the hood."

"Yeah," Augusta said.

"So from that aspect alone, it's really, well, important to keep good working relations with the guys on the squad. But from the other aspect, too, of *liking* most of these guys, though I can't honestly say I'm crazy about Andy Parker, still, he's not too bad a person when you understand him, from *that* aspect I'd really like them to be there to share my wedding with me. You understand, Gus?"

"Yeah," she said, and sighed. "Well, Bert, then I guess we'll just have to figure on more people than we did originally."

"How many did we figure originally?"

"About seventy, seventy-five."

"Maybe we can still keep it down to that."

"I don't see how," Augusta said.

"Well, let's look at that list again, okay?"

They looked at the list again. He did not mention to her that tomorrow morning he would begin questioning a dozen or more known sex offenders. They talked only about the wedding. Then they went out to brunch, and strolled the city. There were outdoor flea markets, and sidewalk art exhibits, and even an antiques show with stalls set up against the curbstones of four barricaded city blocks. For a little while it felt like Paris.

On Monday morning he became a cop again.

Three

In the penal law of the state for which Kling worked, all sex offenses were listed under Article 130. PL 130.35, for example, was Rape 1st Degree, which was a Class B felony. PL 130.38 was Consensual Sodomy, a Class B misdemeanor. PL 130.55 was Sexual Abuse 3rd Degree, another Class B misdemeanor. There were eleven separate sex offenses listed under Article 130, which noted, incidentally, that "a person shall not be convicted of any offense defined in this Article, or of an attempt to commit the same, solely on the uncorroborated testimony of the alleged victim, except in the case of Sexual Abuse 3rd Degree." There were some cops who found it amusing that the exception to this note did not also apply to the third definition of Sexual Misconduct, which was "engaging in sexual conduct with an animal or a dead human body," it perhaps being reasonable to assume that neither of these victims could possibly give any testimony at all.

There were other cops who found nothing at all amusing about Article 130. A great many criminals shared their opinion. Sex offenders were the least-respected convicts in any prison society; if a violator of Article 130 could have pretended that he was an ax murderer instead, or an arsonist, or a man who had filled a ditch with fourteen poisoned wives, he'd have preferred that to entering the prison as a sex offender. There had to be something terribly wrong with a man who'd committed a sex crime—*any* sort of sex crime. Or so the reasoning went, inside the walls and outside as well.

When it came to degrees of criminality, there were very few opinions that cops and crooks did not mutually share: Kling, on that Monday morning when he returned to work, found himself questioning these sex offenders with a rising sense of revulsion. Their names had been selected the morning before, and instructions had been left with the desk sergeant to have his uniformed force round them up for questioning first thing Monday morning. They were here now, a baker's dozen of them in the squadroom or waiting outside on benches in the corridor. Carella and Kling were sharing the interrogations. There was not a single man in that squadroom who did not know he was there because a teenage girl had been found murdered and presumably sexually abused last Saturday night. The news had been in all the papers and on all the television shows. If you're a sex offender, you get used to the fact that any time somebody so much as gets felt up in the subway, the cops'll be around to talk to you about it. But this was a big one. This was a homicide.

Kling started each of his interrogations with the exact same words. He told the man sitting opposite him why he was there, and he made certain the man knew he was not being charged with anything. A girl was found murdered, however, and there *had* been indications (he did not reveal *which* indications) that sex may have been a contributing factor, and since the man sitting opposite him was a known offender, Kling would appreciate it if he could account for his whereabouts on Saturday night between the hours of ten-thirty and eleven-thirty. Each of the men invariably (*and* reasonably) protested that just because he'd once taken a fall for Sodomy Three or Rape Two or any one (or more) of the other eleven crimes listed under Article 130, this was no reason for the police to pick him up and drag him into the station house every time some little girl had her skirt lifted. There *was* such a thing as rehabilitation, you know, and it didn't help a man to be constantly reminded of his past errors. Kling immediately apologized for a system that forced a man to carry forever the burden of his criminal record, but if the man could only understand that Kling was trying to establish his *innocence* rather than his guilt, why then, the man would simply excuse the inconvenience and answer the questions and go on about his business.

Sure, the man would invariably say. Until the *next* time.

But he answered the questions.

The fifth man who approached Kling's desk had black wavy hair and blue eyes. He was wearing a navy-blue jacket over a pale-blue sports shirt. His trousers were a dark blue too, but they did not quite match the jacket. Jacket and trousers alike were rumpled, and there was a beard stubble on the man's face. He pulled out the chair opposite Kling and sat immediately.

"Mr. Donatelli?" Kling said.

"Yes, sir," Donatelli said. His voice was low. His pale-blue eyes looked at the filing cabinets, the water cooler, the electric fan, the clock on the squadroom wall, anything but Kling.

"James Donatelli?"

"Yes, sir."

"Mr. Donatelli," Kling said, "have you got any idea why we asked you to come up here?"

"Yes, sir, I suppose it has to do with the little girl who was killed," Donatelli said.

"That's right," Kling said.

"I had nothing to do with that," Donatelli said.

"Good, I'm glad to hear it."

"You know," Donatelli said, "a man takes one fall in his life on an offense of this nature, he's right away listed as some kind of maniac. I had nothing to do with that girl's murder, and I'm happy to be able to tell you that."

"That's good, Mr. Donatelli, because no one's accusing you of anything. I'm sorry we have to inconvenience you this way, but . . ."

"That's all right," Donatelli said, and waved the apology aside with an open hand. "But what is it you want to know? I'd like to get this over with, I'll be losing half a day's pay as it is."

"Can you tell me where you were last Saturday night?" Kling said.

"What time?"

"Between ten-thirty and eleven-thirty."

"Yes, I know exactly where I was," Donatelli said.

"Where was that?"

"I was bowling."

"Where?"

"At the Avenue L Alleys."

"Who were you bowling with?" Kling asked.

"I was bowling alone," Donatelli said, and Kling looked up from his pad, and their eyes met for the first time.

"Alone?" Kling said.

"I know that sounds funny."

"You always bowl alone?"

"No, but my girl friend got sick. And I didn't feel like sitting home, so I went alone."

"Well, that's okay," Kling said, "I'm sure someone at the bowling alley will remember your being there, and can . . ."

"Well, it's the first time I was ever to this particular bowling alley," Donatelli said. "My girl friend is the one suggested it. So I was supposed to meet her there. But she got sick."

"Mm-huh. Well, what's her name? I'll give her a call and . . ."

"She left for California," Donatelli said, and Kling looked up from his pad again, and Donatelli turned his eyes away.

"When did she leave for California?" Kling asked.

"Yesterday. She caught an afternoon plane."

"What's her name?"

"Betsy."

"What's her last name?"

"I don't know her last name."

"I thought she was your girl friend."

"Well, she's only a casual friend. Actually, I met her in the park Saturday afternoon, and she said did I ever go bowling, and I said I hadn't been bowling in a long time, so she said why don't we bowl together tonight. So I said okay, and I arranged to meet her at the Avenue L Alleys at ten o'clock."

"Is that what time you got there?" Kling asked. "Ten?"

"Yes. But she wasn't there."

"She was sick," Kling said.

"Yes."

"How do you *know* she was sick?"

"What? Oh, there was a message for me. When I got there, the manager said Betsy had called and left a message."

"I see. When you came in, the manager said Betsy had left a message for James Donatelli . . ."

"Jimmy Donatelli."

"Jimmy Donatelli, and the message was she was sick and couldn't make it."

"Yes."

"Then the manager knows your name, right?"

"What?"

"The manager. Of the bowling alley. The Avenue L Alleys. If he took a message for you, he knows your name. He'll remember you."

"Well . . ."

"Yes, what is it, Mr. Donatelli?" Kling said.

"Well . . . I'm not sure he'll remember my name," Donatelli said. "Because it was the first time I'd ever been there, you see."

"Mm-huh," Kling said. "What happened when you walked in on Saturday night? It was about ten o'clock, is that what you said?"

"Yes, ten o'clock."

"So what happened when you walked in? Did the manager ask if you were Jimmy Donatelli?"

"Yes, that's exactly what he asked."

"Was he asking everybody?"

"No. Oh, I see what you mean. No. Betsy had given him a description of me. Black hair and blue eyes. So when I walked in, the manager saw my hair and my eyes, and he naturally asked if I was Jimmy Donatelli."

"What'd he say then?"

"He gave me the message. That Betsy was sick."

"So you decided to stay and bowl alone."

"Yes."

"Instead of going over to see her."

"Well, I didn't know where she lived."

"That's right, you didn't even know her last name."

"That's right. I *still* don't."

"So you stayed and bowled. What time did you leave the alleys?"

"It must've been around midnight."

"You bowled till midnight. From ten to midnight. Alone."

"Yes."

"Didn't it get boring?"

"Yes."

"But you stayed there and bowled."

"Yes."

"Then what?"

"I went home."

"And yesterday afternoon Betsy left for California."

"Yes."

"How do you know?"

"Well, she called me."

"Oh, she had your phone number."

"Yes."

"Why didn't she call to tell you she was sick? On Saturday night, I mean. Why'd she call the bowling alley instead?"

"I guess she tried to reach me, but I'd probably left already."

"And you didn't think to ask her last name, huh?

When she called to say she was leaving for California."

"Well, she was just a casual acquaintance, I figured I'd never see her again."

"How old is she, this Betsy?"

"Oh, she's old *enough,* don't worry about that."

"Because I notice on your card here . . ."

"Yes, you don't have to worry about that," Donatelli said. "I know what it says on my card, that was a long time ago. You don't have to worry about anything like that. Besides, this was only supposed to be some innocent bowling, you know, so really there's . . ."

"Let's run over to the bowling alley, huh?" Kling said.

"What for?"

"See if the manager remembers you."

"I doubt if he'll remember me."

"Well, who the hell *is* going to remember you?" Kling asked. "You're giving me an alibi nobody can back, now what do you expect me to do, huh? I told you up front that a girl was murdered Saturday night, you know that's why you're in here, now what the hell do you expect me to believe, Mr. Donatelli? That you were bowling alone for two goddamn hours because you got stood up by somebody whose name you don't know and who conveniently leaves for California the next day? Now come on, willya?"

"Well, that's the truth," Donatelli said.

"Steve," Kling called. "You want to step over here a minute?"

Carella had just finished interrogating a man at his own desk, and he was standing now and stretching while waiting for the next man to be shown in. He walked to where Kling and Donatelli were sitting.

"This is Detective Carella," Kling said. "Would you mind telling him the story you just told me?"

Some ten minutes later Donatelli changed his story.

They had moved from the squadroom to the Interrogation Room down the hall, and Donatelli was telling them about how he'd been stood up by the mysterious California-bound Betsy whom he'd met in the park on Saturday afternoon. Carella suddenly said, "*How* old did you say this girl was?"

"Oh, at least nineteen, twenty," Donatelli said.

"How old are *you?*" Carella asked.

"I'm forty-six, sir."

"That's picking them kind of young, isn't it?"

"He's picked them younger than that," Kling said. "Take a look at the card, Steve."

"Well, that was a long time ago," Donatelli said.

"Sodomy One," Carella said.

"Yes, but that was a long time ago."

"With a ten-year-old girl," Carella said.

"Well . . ."

"I've got a daughter almost ten," Carella said.

"Well."

"So how old was this Betsy? The one you were supposed to bowl with Saturday night?"

"I told you. Nineteen, twenty. Anyway, that's how old she *looked.* I only met her that afternoon, I didn't ask to see her I.D. card."

"Fellow with a record like yours," Carella said, "you ought to make a *practice* of asking to see the I.D."

"Well, she looked about nineteen, twenty."

"Yes, but how old *was* she?" Carella said.

"Well, how would I know? I never even saw her again."

"Because she got sick, huh?"

"Yes."

"And called the bowling alley to leave a message for you."

"Yes."

"And then left for California the next day."

"Yes."

"Where in California?"

"San Francisco, I think she said. Or maybe Los Angeles."

"Or maybe San Diego," Kling said.

"Well, no, it was either San Francisco or Los Angeles."

"If that was where she was going," Carella said, "and if she left yesterday . . ."

"That's when she left, sir," Donatelli said.

"We can check with the airlines. There aren't that many late-afternoon flights to California, and there couldn't have been too many girls named Betsy . . ."

"Well, I'm not even sure it was California," Donatelli said.

"Mr. Donatelli," Carella said, "are you aware of the fact that we're talking about a homicide here? Are you aware of that? Are you sure you realize that a girl was brutally murdered on Saturday night and that . . . ?"

"Yes, I'm aware of it, I realize it."

"Then why are you giving us this bullshit about a bowling alley, and a girl you met in the park, now what is *that* supposed to be, Mr. Donatelli? Are we supposed to *believe* that goddamn story? If you want my advice—I'm not supposed to give you this kind of advice, Mr. Donatelli—I'd get a lawyer in here right away, because the bullshit you're giving us, it sounds to me like you're going to be in very serious trouble before too long. Now that's my advice."

"I don't need a lawyer," Donatelli said. "I didn't kill that girl you're talking about."

"Mr. Donatelli," Carella said, "I think we're going to have to hold you in custody, in what amounts to something more than a routine interrogation, and that being the case, I'll have to advise you of your rights. In keeping with the Supreme Court decision in Miranda versus Arizona, we are not permitted to ask you any questions until you are warned of your right to counsel and your privilege against self-incrimination. First, you have the right to remain silent if you so choose. Do you understand that?"

"Yes."

"Second, you do not have to answer any police questions if you don't want to. Do you understand that?"

"Yes."

"Third, if you *do* decide to answer any questions, the answers may be used as evidence against you. Do you understand that?"

"Yes."

"You have the right to consult with an attorney before or during police questioning. If you do not have the money to hire a lawyer, a lawyer will be appointed to consult with you. Do you understand everything I've told you?"

"Yes, I understand."

"Are you willing to answer questions without an attorney here to counsel you?"

"Yes," Donatelli said. "I didn't kill that girl."

"Then what *did* you do?" Carella asked at once. He was able to question Donatelli more freely now; the man had signified that he understood all the warnings, and had waived his right to have an attorney present. This did not give the police license to keep him there for four days and four nights while successive teams of interrogators bludgeoned him with questions. As a matter of fact, if Donatelli changed his mind at any point during the questioning, he could simply say, "I don't want to answer any more questions," and that would be that; the police would have to respect his wishes and cease all questioning at once. In many respects, America is a very nice country.

"I didn't do anything," Donatelli said.

"Where were you on Saturday night? And please skip the bowling-alley bullshit, if you don't mind."

"I told you where I was."

"We don't believe you."

"Well, that's where I was."

"If you're hiding something, Mr. Donatelli, it can't be anything as serious as this homicide, I'm sure you realize that. So if you're hiding something, I suggest you tell us about it, because otherwise we're going to start thinking things you don't want us to think, and then you'd better change your mind and get a lawyer in here to help you. What do you say?"

"I can't tell you where I was Saturday night."

"Then you *weren't* at the bowling alley, huh?"

"I didn't say that."

"Where were you?"

"I can't tell you that."

"Why not?"

"Because if I tell you that . . . no, I can't tell you that."

"Mr. Donatelli, we've got an eyewitness to the murder. We've got a girl who can identify the man who killed Muriel Stark. Now we can bring that girl up here, Mr. Donatelli. We can have a car pick her up, and she'll be here in five minutes flat, and we can ask her to identify that man for us, we'll put him in a line-up with six detectives and ask her to pick out the man who killed her cousin. Do you want us to do that, Mr. Donatelli, or do you want to tell us where you were on Saturday night between ten-thirty and eleven-thirty?"

"Well, I . . . I wasn't at the bowling alley," Donatelli said.

"Where were you?"

"With a girl."

"What girl?"

"A girl I know."

"Betsy?"

"No. I made Betsy up."

"Then what girl?"

"Well, what's the use?" Donatelli said.

"Who's the girl, Mr. Donatelli?"

"It won't help me. If I tell you who she is, it won't help me."

"Why not?"

"Because she'll lie. She'll say she doesn't know me."

"Why would she do that?"

"It's what I told her to say. I told her if ever anyone asks her about me—her mother, her father, a policeman, *anyone*—what I want her to say is she's never even heard of me."

"Why's that, Mr. Donatelli?"

"Well," Donatelli said, and shrugged.
"How old is this girl?" Carella asked.
"Well," Donatelli said.
"How old is she?"
"She's pretty young," Donatelli said.
"*How* young?"
"She's thirteen."

Carella turned away, walked toward the far end of the narrow room, and then came back to where Donatelli was sitting.

"Were you with her Saturday night?"
"Yes."
"Where?"
"Her house."
"Where were her parents?"
"They went to a movie."
"What time did you go up there?"
"At about ten."
"And what time did you leave her?"
"At a quarter to twelve."
"What's her name?"

"It doesn't matter," Donatelli said. "If I give you her name, and you ask her about me, she'll say she doesn't know me. She knows I can get in trouble for being with her, she knows that. She'll lie."

"What's her name?"
"What difference does it make?"
"What's her goddamn *name!*"
"Gloria Hanley."
"Where does she live?"
"831 North Sheridan."
"How long have you known her?"
"I met her six months ago."
"How old was she then?"
"Well, I . . . I suppose she was twelve."

"You're a very nice man, Mr. Donatelli," Carella said.

"I love her," Donatelli said.

The object of Mr. Donatelli's affections was eating a peanut butter and jelly sandwich when she opened the door to the apartment on North Sheridan. Gloria Hanley was a tall, angular girl with tiny breasts, boyish hips, green eyes, a dusting of freckles on her cheeks, and sun-washed blonde hair cut in a Dutch Boy bob. They had announced themselves as police officers, and she had asked them to hold up their shields to the peephole before she would open the door. She stood in the open doorway now in jeans and short-sleeved blouse, studying them with only mild interest.

"I was just having lunch," she said. "What is it?"

"We'd like to ask you some questions," Carella said. "Would it be all right if we came in?"

"This isn't about that dope thing, is it?" Gloria said.

"What dope thing?"

"At school. Some kids were caught smoking dope in the toilet."

"No, this isn't about that."

"Well, sure, come on in," Gloria said. "I hope you won't mind my eating while we talk. I go to school at the crack of dawn, you see, the bus picks me up at six-thirty, would you believe it? But I get *home* early, too, so I guess it's not all that horrible. The thing is I'm positively *starved* when I get here. Would *you* care for something to eat?"

"Thank you, no," Carella said.

They followed her into the kitchen. Gloria poured herself a glass of milk and drank half of it before she sat down at the table. "My mother should be home any minute," she said, "if this is anything she ought to hear. She works part-time, usually gets home a little after I do. What's this all about, anyway?"

"Gloria, I wonder if you can tell us where you were last Saturday night between ten and midnight."

"Huh?" Gloria said.

"Last Saturday night," Carella said. "That would have been Saturday, the sixth."

"Gee, I don't know *where* I was," Gloria said.

"Would you have been here?"

"Home, you mean?"

"Yes. Here in the apartment."

"Yeah, I guess so," Gloria said.

"Was anyone with you?"

"My parents, I guess."

"Your parents were here with you?"

"Or maybe not. Saturday night, huh? No, wait a minute, they went out, that's right."

"Where'd they go?"

"A movie, I think. I'm not sure. Yeah, a movie. Mm-huh. You sure you don't want something to eat?"

"Were you here alone?" Kling asked.

"I guess so. If my parents were out, then I guess I was here alone."

"Any of your friends stop by to see you?" Carella asked.

"Not that I can remember."

"Well, this was only Saturday night," Carella said. "It shouldn't really be too difficult to remember whether . . ."

"No, I'm pretty sure nobody stopped by," Gloria said.

"So you were here alone."

"Yes."

"What'd you do?"

"Watched television, I guess."

"Alone?"

"Yes."

"Gloria, do you know a man named James Donatelli?"

"No, I don't believe so," Gloria said, and poured more milk from the container into her glass.

"He says he knows you."

"Really? James *who* did you say?"

"Donatelli."

"No," she said, and shook her head. "I don't know him. He must be mistaken."

"He says he was here Saturday night."

"Here? You're kidding. I was here alone."

"Then he *wasn't* here, is that right?"

"I don't even know who you're talking about."

"James Donatelli."

"Nobody by that name was here Saturday night. Or any *other* night, for that matter."

"He said you might lie for him."

"Why should I lie for somebody I don't even know?"

"So he won't go back to prison."

"I don't *know* anybody who's been in prison. You're making a mistake. Officers, really, I mean it. I don't know this man, whoever he is."

"Gloria, a girl was killed on Saturday night . . ."

"Well, I'm sorry, but . . ."

"Please hear me out. This man Donatelli has a prison record, we picked him up this morning because we wanted to question him about the murder."

"I don't know him, I'm sorry."

"He says he was here Saturday night. That's his alibi, Gloria. He was here at the time the girl was killed."

"Well, that's . . . Is that what he told you?"

"Yes. And he also said you'd deny it."

"Well, he was right, I *am* denying it. He wasn't here."

"That means he hasn't got an alibi."

"I'm sorry about that, but how can I say he was here if he wasn't here?"

"Gloria, we're going to have to assume that Donatelli was lying to us. Which means we're going to keep questioning him about where he *really* was on Saturday night. And if we *still* can't get some satisfactory answers, we'll run a line-up on him and try to get a positive identification from the girl who witnessed the murder."

"Well, if he didn't do it, he's got nothing to worry about," Gloria said.

"Before we put him through all that, I want to ask you again—are you *sure* you don't know anyone named James Donatelli?"

"I'm positive."

"No one by that name was here on Saturday night."

"No one. I was here alone. I was here alone watching television."

"Gloria," Carella said, "if you know this man, please say so."

"I do not know him," she said.

At two o'clock that afternoon they ran a line-up in the squadroom. Six detectives and James Donatelli stood in a row. The detectives all had dark hair and light eyes, and they were all wearing dark suits and shirts without ties. None of them wore hats. James Donatelli was the third man in the line, flanked by two detectives on his left, and four detectives on his right. In addition to the seven men in the line-up, there were three other men in the room: Carella, Kling, and a man named Israel Mandelbaum who had been appointed as Donatelli's attorney, and who *still* objected to the line-up, even though Donatelli had agreed to it.

"You'll get a person in here," Mandelbaum said, "she won't remember *what* the hell she saw Saturday night, she'll pick you out of the line-up, you'll spend the rest of your life in jail. You want to go to jail for the rest of your life?"

"I won't go to jail," Donatelli said. "I'm innocent. I was with Gloria at the time of the murder. I'm not the man, I'm not the guilty party."

Mandelbaum shook his head gravely, and said, "If I had a nickel for every poor slob who was ever mistakenly identified in a line-up, I'd be a rich man and not a practicing lawyer."

"Don't worry about it," Donatelli said, but Mandelbaum was still shaking his head when Patricia Lowery walked into the squadroom.

Both of her hands were bandaged, and there was a bandage on her left cheek as well, where eight stitches had been taken to close the knife wound there. Carella led her to a chair and then asked if she'd care for a cup of coffee or anything. She declined the coffee. She was already looking over the men lined up in front of the detention cage. She knew why she was there; Carella had prepared her on the telephone.

"Patricia," he said now, "there are seven men standing across the room there. Would you please go over to them, and look at them closely, and then tell me whether you recognize any one of them."

Patricia got out of the chair and walked slowly across the room, past the filing cabinets and over to where the seven men were standing just in front of the detention cage. She paused before each man, looking at him carefully before she moved on to the next man in line. When she reached the end of the line, she turned to Carella and said, "Yes, I recognize one of these men."

"Where did you see this man before?" Carella asked.

"He murdered my cousin last Saturday night," Patricia said. "And he cut me on the hands and on the face."

"Would you please indicate who this man is by walking to him and placing your hand on his shoulder?"

Patricia turned and walked toward the line of men again.

Her hand reached out.

The man whose shoulder she touched was a detective who'd been on the force for seventeen years, and who'd been transferred to the 87th Squad only the month before. His name was Walt Lefferts.

Four

The detectives weren't too terribly surprised. Disappointed, yes, but not surprised. Even Walt Lefferts, who'd been mistakenly identified as the killer, wasn't surprised. They were all experienced cops and familiar with the unreliability of witnesses. At the Police Academy, in fact, they had all sat through a variation of what was known as the "Window Washer Bit." During a lecture unrelated to identification or witnesses or testimony, a man would unobtrusively come into the room, cross quietly behind the instructor and then go to the window, where he would busy himself working on a latch there. The man had brown hair. He was wearing brown trousers, a blue jacket, and brown shoes. He was carrying nothing but a screwdriver. He would work on the window for five minutes, and then cross quietly behind the instructor again and let himself out of the room. The moment he was gone, the instructor would interrupt his lecture and ask the students to describe this man who had just been in the room for five minutes. Specifically, he wanted to know:

(1) The color of the man's hair.
(2) The color of his trousers.
(3) The color of his jacket.
(4) The color of his shoes.
(5) What he was carrying, if anything.

(6) What he did while in the room.

Well, the color of the man's hair was variously described by the students as black, brown, blond, red, and bald. (Some said he was wearing a hat.) Thirty percent of the students correctly identified the color of the trousers as brown, but an equal percentage said they were blue. The remainder of the students opted for beige or gray. As for the man's blue jacket, it was described in descending order of preference as brown, green, gray, blue, tan, and yellow. The brown shoes were described by most of the students as black. When it came to what the man was carrying, an astonishing sixty-two percent of the students said a bucket of water. Presumably, this was because a similar percentage reported that he had washed the windows while in the room. Only four percent of the students reported accurately that he had been carrying a screwdriver and that he had worked on a window latch while in the room. One student said he was carrying a stepladder. It was probably this same student who said the man had changed a light bulb while in the room. And another student (but he'd undoubtedly been asleep during the lecture) said he had not seen anyone entering the room at all!

So Patricia Lowery's unreliability wasn't totally unexpected. In fact, that's why they'd run a line-up in the first place. They could have done it another way. They could have put Donatelli in the Interrogation Room, facing the one-way mirror. Then they could have brought Patricia into the room next door and asked her to look through the glass. Then they could have said, "Is that the man who killed your cousin?" But they knew too many rape and/or assault victims were ready to identify *anyone* as their attacker, a response generated more by confusion and fear than by vindictiveness or outrage. The line-up was safer.

When they told Patricia Lowery that Walt Lefferts was a Detective 2nd/Grade, she would not believe them. She insisted that he was the man who'd killed her cousin. She had been standing not three feet away from the murderer, she had watched him wielding the knife, she had seen him approaching her after he'd finished with Muriel, she certainly knew what he looked like, she would never in her life forget what he looked like. They explained again that Walt Lefferts was a detective, and that he'd been home in bed with his wife of thirteen summers on the night of the murder. Patricia said it was amazing. He looked so much like the man, it was positively amazing. They thanked her for coming up to the squadroom, and then they sent her home in a radio motor patrol car.

There was something that had to be established before they could continue with the investigation. Until now they had been working on the supposition that Patricia Lowery could identify the man who had slain her cousin. Her false identification of Walt Lefferts opened up a whole new can of buttered beans. The question they now asked was: Had she actually seen the man? It was one thing to have seen him and then to have become confused about what he looked like. It was quite another not to have seen him at all. She had told them he was "a perfect stranger," but if she hadn't really seen him, how the hell could she know *what* he was?

As soon as it was dark, they went back to the tenement on Harding and Fourteenth. In their first conversation with Patricia Lowery, they had asked, "Would you recognize him if you saw him again?" and she had replied, "Yes. There wasn't any light in the hallway, but there was light from the streetlamp." There was indeed a streetlamp outside the building on Harding Avenue, but its globe and its light bulb had been shattered, and the area of sidewalk directly in front of the building was in darkness. They climbed the steps and entered the building. The hallway was so black, they had trouble seeing each other, even standing side by side. They waited, reasoning that their eyes would grow accustomed to the dark, but the blackness was so total that even after standing there for ten minutes, Carella could barely discern Kling's features. There had been no moon on the night of the murder; by Patricia's own report, it had been raining heavily. If the streetlamp outside had been inoperative, Patricia couldn't possibly have seen anyone clearly enough to have identified him. If, on the other hand, the streetlamp had been burning . . .

In this city, patrolmen were required to report lamp outages observed during the night. The printed form called for the location of the lamp, the lamppost number, the time the lamp went out (if known), the time the lamp was relighted, and whether it was the globe, the bulb, or the mantle that had been broken—the patrolman was to indicate this by putting a check mark in the appropriate space. At the bottom of the form, the words ACTION TAKEN were printed, and there were three blank lines beneath those words. The patrolman was supposed to indicate on those lines whether he had taken any special action short of climbing the pole and replacing the light bulb himself. Normally—unless the lamppost was just outside a bank or a jewelry store or some other establishment that was a prime target for a nighttime burglary—the patrolman took no action other than to turn in the outage report at the completion of his tour. The desk sergeant then notified the electric company, which got around to repairing the lamp in its own sweet time—the very next day, or three days later, or in some sections of the city, two or three *weeks* later.

Patrolman Shanahan, who had discovered Muriel Stark's body, had not turned in a lamp outage report after his tour of duty that Saturday night, but perhaps he'd been too busy reporting the homicide. Patrolman Feeny, on the other hand, had walked that same beat on Friday night's graveyard shift. And when he'd reported back to the station house at eight o'clock Saturday morning, he had handed a lamp outage report to the desk sergeant, and on it he had indicated that the precinct was the 87th, the precinct post was post number 3, and the date was September 6. He had located the lamppost at the corner of Harding and Fourteenth, and had identified it as lamppost number 6—there were six lampposts on the block, three on each side of the street. He had not indicated when the lamp went out, presumably because he hadn't known. Nor had he written in a time for when the lamp had been restored to service. He had put check marks alongside the words Broken Globe and also Broken Bulb. There were no comments under ACTION TAKEN. He had signed the bottom of the form with his rank, his name, and his shield number. The report told Carella that the light had been out on Friday night, and he knew from his visit to the scene that the light was out *now* as well. What he did *not* know was whether it had been repaired sometime after the Friday outage, and then broken again after the Saturday night murder.

He immediately called the electric company.

The man who answered the phone said, "Yes, that outage was reported."

"When was it repaired?" Carella asked.

"Look, you know how many damn outages we get in this city every night of the week?" the man asked.

"I only want to know about this particular outage," Carella said. "Lamppost number 6, on the corner of Fourteenth and Harding. According to what we've got here, our patrolman reported a broken bulb and globe on the morning of Saturday, September 6, and presumably the desk sergeant . . ."

"Yes, it was reported to us. I already told you it was reported."

"Was it repaired?"

"I would have to check that."

"Please check it," Carella said. "I'm specifically interested in knowing whether it had been repaired by eleven o'clock that Saturday night."

"Just a second."

Carella waited.

When the man came back onto the line, he said,

"Yes, that lamp was repaired at four fifty-seven P.M. on Saturday, September 6."

"It's out again now," Carella said.

"Well, so what? If you didn't happen to know it, that lamp happens to be right outside an abandoned building that's being torn down. You're lucky we repaired the damn thing at all."

"I'd like it repaired again," Carella said. "We're investigating a homicide here, and it's important for us to know whether that streetlamp could have illuminated . . ."

"Well, shit, put your *own* emergency service on it."

"No, I want it fixed the way the electric company would have fixed it. Your light bulb, your globe."

"Who's this I'm talking to?"

"Detective Carella."

"*Paisan,* have a heart, huh? I'm up to my *ass* in orders here. I'll be lucky if I get through them by the Fourth of . . ."

"I need that lamp fixed," Carella said. He looked up at the wall clock. "It's a quarter past seven," he said. "My partner and I are going out for a bite, we'll be back at the scene there by eight, eight-thirty. I want it fixed by then."

"You sure you're Italian?" the man from the electric company said, and hung up.

Carella buzzed the desk sergeant, asked for Patrolman Shanahan's home number, and immediately dialed it. Shanahan barked "Hello!" into the phone, and then immediately apologized when Carella identified himself. He said his sixteen-year-old daughter kept getting phone calls day and night from her girl friends or from these pimply-faced jerks who kept coming to the house, man couldn't get a moment's peace, phone going like sixty all the time.

"So I'm sorry for snapping your head off," he said.

"That's okay," Carella said. "There was just one thing I wanted to ask you. On Saturday night, when you found that girl's body . . ."

"Damn shame," Shanahan said.

"... would you remember whether the streetlamp was working?"

"Sure, it was working."

"How do you know?"

"Well, I just know it was working. I automatically look for outages, know what I mean? I see a busted lamp, I fill out a report. But aside from that, I could see the girl's hand. Up on the top step there, know what I mean? Now if the lamp had been out, it would've been blacker'n a witch's asshole on that corner. Couldn't have seen the hand, know what I mean? But I could see it. Laying palm up, right there outside the doorway. Didn't put my flashlight on till after I'd climbed the steps. Threw my beam inside the doorway then and saw the body."

"Did you see anything inside the hallway *before* you turned on your flash?"

"I could see the outline of the body, yes. I knew there was a body inside there, yes."

"Okay, thanks a lot," Carella said.

"Don't mention it," Shanahan said.

At a quarter past eight that Monday night, Carella and Kling went back to Harding Avenue. The streetlamp was burning again. It cast a circle of light onto the sidewalk and into the gutter. The circle of light included the entire front stoop of the building in which Muriel Stark had been murdered. The detectives went into the hallway. The only light was the bounce from the lamp outside, but on the floor they could clearly make out the chalked outline of Muriel Stark's body, and on the walls they could see scribbled graffiti and spatters they assumed were bloodstains. Standing against the wall opposite Kling, Carella could even distinguish the color of his eyes. There was no question but that the reflected light in that hallway was sufficient for identification. They *had* to believe that Patricia Lowery had indeed seen a dark-haired, blue-eyed man stabbing her cousin to death. This being the case, they further had to believe that she'd mistakenly identified Walt Lefferts only because he resembled the killer more closely than any of the other men in the line-up. They realized with dismay that Patricia's value to them had been totally destroyed by this false identification. They were looking for a dark-haired, blue-eyed man who looked like Walt Lefferts, yes, but even if they found him, and even if Patricia pointed an accusing finger at him, how could they know for certain that he was the man she'd *really* seen committing the murder? She had *also* seen Walt Lefferts committing the murder, hadn't she?

As far as they were concerned, they were still looking for someone Patricia had described—accurately, it now seemed —as "a perfect stranger."

The kids knew somebody had been killed in that building on Saturday night, but this was Tuesday afternoon and the barricades the City Housing Authority had put up on either end of the block made the street perfect for stickball. It was still early September, and there'd be plenty of daylight before dinnertime. So they congregated at about four o'clock, chose up their sides and chalked their bases onto the asphalt, and got down to the serious business at hand.

The boy playing center field was standing almost directly opposite the hallway in which Muriel Stark had been found. He wasn't thinking about Muriel Stark, he didn't even *know* Muriel Stark. As a matter of fact, he wasn't thinking about murder or sex maniacs or anything but how hard and how far the batter on the other team would hit the rubber ball. They had two guys on base now, and a hit would put them ahead. This was a tense moment, much more important than who had got killed in the building on Saturday night, or who had done it. The boy saw the pitcher on his team wind up and fling the ball toward the other team's batter. The ball bounced on the asphalt paving, came up toward the batter waist-high. The broomstick handle came around in a powerful swing, the narrow round of wood colliding with the rubber ball and sending it soaring over the pitcher's head, and then the second baseman's head, to bounce somewhere between second base and center field. The boy came running in, glove low. The ball was still bouncing, and he was running to meet it, the way he'd been taught—run to meet the ball, don't wait for it to come to you. It took a bad hop some four feet from his glove, veered off to the right and rolled into the sewer at the curb.

"That's only a double!" he shouted immediately. "That's only a double, it went down the sewer."

There was no argument, they all knew the rules. The batter grumbled a little about losing a sure homer, but rules were rules and the ball had rolled down the sewer and that made it an automatic double. They gathered around the sewer grating now, half a dozen of them. Two of them seized opposite sides of the grating, their hands reaching down to clasp the cast-iron crossbars, and they lifted the grating and moved it onto the pavement, and then the smallest boy in the group lowered himself into the sewer.

"You see it?" somebody asked.

"Yeah, it's over there," the boy answered.

"So get it already."

"Just a second, I can't *reach* the damn thing."

"What's that over there?" somebody else asked.

"Let me get the ball first, okay?"

"Over there. That shiny thing."

They had found the murder weapon.

Or, to be more exact, they had found a knife near the scene of a murder, and they immediately turned it over to the police.

The blade of the knife was three and three-quarter inches long. It was a paring knife, with a pointed tip and a razor-sharp stainless-steel blade. Two stainless-steel rivets held the blade fastened to the curved wooden handle, which was itself four and a half inches long. The overall length of the knife, from the end of the wooden handle to the pointed tip of the blade, was eight and a quarter inches. The rain had washed the blade clean of any blood, but blood had soaked into the wooden handle and stained it, and it was this that the laboratory reported on.

There were two types of blood on the handle of the knife. O and A. Presumably Muriel's and Patricia's. And presumably the killer had first slain Muriel, and then slashed Patricia, and then—instead of pursuing her when she'd run away from the building—had come down the steps to the curb and thrown the murder weapon into the sewer.

There were no usable fingerprints on the handle of the knife.

The funeral took place on Wednesday afternoon.

From the funeral home on Twelfth and Ascot, the black limousines drove out to the cemetery on Sands Spit. There were six limousines, and behind them a row of family cars with their headlights on, and behind those one of the 87th Precinct's unmarked sedans. Carella was at the wheel, Kling was riding shotgun beside him. The day was one of those September miracles that made living in this part of the country almost worthwhile. The black cars moved slowly against a sky blown clear of clouds, utterly blue and dazzling with light. There was not the slightest trace of summer lingering on the air; the bite promised imminent autumn, threatened winter on the distant horizon.

At the cemetery, they walked from the cars to the open hole in the ground where the coffin was poised on canvas straps, waiting to be lowered hydraulically into the earth. A pair of gravediggers stood by silently, leaning on their shovels, hats in their hands. The Lowerys were Catholic, and the priest and clergy stood by the coffin now, waiting for the mourners to make their way along the gravel path to the burial site. Overhead, a pair of jays, blue against the bluer sky, cawed as though resenting intrusion. When the family and friends had gathered around the open grave, the priest sprinkled the coffin and the grave with holy water, and then incensed both, and said, in prayer, "Dearest brothers, let us faithfully and lovingly remember our sister, whom God has taken to himself from the trials of this world. Lord, have mercy."

"Christ, have mercy," the chanter of the first choir said.

"Lord, have mercy," the second choir responded.

"Our Father," the priest said, and sprinkled the coffin again, "who art in heaven, hallowed be thy name. Thy kingdom come, thy will be done on earth as it is in heaven. Give us this day our daily bread and lead us not into temptation . . ."

"But deliver us from evil."

"From the gate of hell."

"Rescue her soul, O Lord."

"May she rest in peace."

"Amen."

"O Lord, hear my prayer," the priest said.

"And let my cry come to you."

"The Lord be with you."

"And with your spirit."

"Let us pray," the priest said. "O Lord, we implore you to grant this mercy to your dead servant, that she who held fast to your will by her intentions, may not receive punishment in return for her deeds; so that, as the true faith united her with the throng of the faithful on earth, your mercy may unite her with the company of the choir of angels in heaven. Through Christ our Lord."

"Amen."

And then it was straight out of *Hamlet*.

Like some grief-stricken Laertes, he threw himself upon the coffin just as it was being lowered into the grave. Carella recognized him at once as the slender, dark-haired, dark-eyed young man whose photograph had been in Patricia Lowery's wallet. He was identified by name in the next moment when a dark-haired woman standing alongside the grave shouted "Andy, no!" and reached over to pull him from the descending casket. Someone shouted an order, the coffin stopped and hung trembling on canvas straps, the young man spread-eagled and sobbing on its shining black lid. The woman was tugging at his arm, trying to break his embrace on the long black box.

"Get away from me, Mom!" he shouted, and a terrible keening moan sprang from his lips in the next moment, his arms hugging the casket, his head thrown back, his cry of inconsolable grief rising to frighten even the jays, who responded in terrified flapping clamor. A man broke from the crowd of mourners, the cast was being identified for Carella without benefit of program—Andrew Lowery on the coffin hanging suspended over the open grave, his mother, Mrs. Lowery, still tugging at his arm, and now a man whom Mrs. Lowery addressed as Frank, and to whom she immediately said, "Help me, your son's gone crazy!" Mother, father, grief-stricken son, and Patricia Lowery standing by and watching her blood relatives with strangely detached eyes, as though they were somehow embarrassing her with their excessive display of emotion. For whereas Andrew Lowery may not have gone quite crazy, he was certainly putting on a fine show of what Hamlet might have called emphatic grief, his phrases of sorrow conjuring the wandering stars and making them stand like wonder-wounded hearers, so to speak. He was pounding on the coffin with his fists now, and shouting, "Muriel, wake up! Muriel, say you're not dead! Muriel, I love you!" while his father and mother tried to pull him off the casket, fearful that he *and* it would tumble into the grave together, the priest hastily muttering a prayer for those resting in the cemetery (or at least *trying* to rest with all the noise Andrew Lowery was making), this time in Latin for the sake of any Roman spectators, *"Oremus. Deus, cuius miseratione animae fidelium,"* and so on.

For a moment Carella wondered whether he should step in and break up the near-riot at graveside. But finally Frank Lowery managed to pull his son off the coffin, and Mrs. Lowery clutched him to her in embrace and shouted, "We all loved her, oh, dear God, we *all* loved her!" and the priest concluded his Latin prayer with the words *"Per eundem Christum, Dominum nostrum."* The gravediggers—who, like cops, had seen it all and heard it all—simply pressed the button that again sent the coffin *de*scending and the soul hopefully *as*cending. The skies above were still as blue as though a jousting tournament were to take place that very afternoon, with banners and pennoncels flying, and shields ablaze with two lions gules on an azure field, and lovely maidens in long pointed hats with silken tassels and merry eyes —rather than eyes red with mourning, or squinched in embarrassment, or narrowed in pain.

"She came to live with us when her parents died," Mrs. Lowery said. "She was fifteen at the time, they were both killed in an automobile accident on the Pennsylvania Turnpike—my sister, Pauline, and my brother-in-law, Mike. Muriel came to live with us a month later. I never adopted her, but I was planning to. She always called me Aunt Lillian, but she was like a daughter to me. And certainly like a sister to Andy and Patricia."

Lillian Lowery carried a bottle of whiskey to the kitchen table and set it down before the detectives. In the other room, her husband Frank was talking to well-wishers who had come back to the house after the funeral.

"I know you're not allowed to drink on duty," she said, "but I feel the need for one myself, and I'd appreciate it if you joined me."

"Thank you," Carella said.

She poured three shot glasses full to their brims. Carella and Kling waited for her to lift her glass, and then they lifted theirs as well. "Andy will miss her most," Mrs. Lowery said, and tilted the glass, swallowing all the whiskey in it. Carella and Kling sipped at their drinks. When Carella put his glass down on the kitchen table, Kling put his down too. "They were really like brother and sister," she said, pouring herself another shot from the bottle. "Except that brothers and sisters sometimes argue. Not Andy and Muriel." She shook her head, lifted the glass, and downed the whiskey. "Never. I never heard a word of anger between them. Never even a raised voice. They got along beautifully. Well, you saw him at the cemetery, he was beside himself with grief. It's going to take him a long time to get over this. He blames himself a little, I think."

"Why do you say that, Mrs. Lowery?" Carella asked.

"Well, he was supposed to go with them to the party, you know. At Paul's house. Paul Gaddis. He's one of Andy's friends. It was his birthday they were celebrating that night. But then at the last minute, Andy got a call from the restaurant, asking if he could come in, so he went to work instead of the party. Even so, he could maybe have saved her, if only he'd been a few minutes earlier."

"I'm not sure I understand you," Carella said.

"Well, he went to pick up the girls."

"Who did? Your son?"

"Yes. Andy."

"If he was working . . ."

"Well, he called here from the restaurant and asked if they were home yet. This was about ten-fifteen. I told him they weren't here, and he said he was through at the restaurant, there'd been a very small crowd for a Saturday night, and he thought he'd head over to Paul's and pick them up. So I said fine. But what happened, you see, Andy went over to Paul's house, and the girls had already left." She shook her head, and poured herself another shot glass full of whiskey.

"Mrs. Lowery," Carella said, "what did Andy do when he got to the party and found out the girls had gone?"

"He went looking for them."

"In the street?"

"Yes. But it began raining again, and he thought they might have gone back to the party, so he went back there. But they weren't there, so he went out looking for them again, and he still couldn't find them. He got here alone at about twelve-fifteen, which is when I called the police. He was soaking wet. You'd have thought he'd taken a shower with his clothes on."

The detectives had gone to the funeral for two reasons. To begin with, they knew that killers sometimes attended the funeral services of their victims, and they wanted to make certain there were no dark-haired, blue-eyed strangers in the crowd. Second, they wanted to show the suspect knife to Patricia Lowery and ask her to identify it as the murder weapon. They had not had a chance to talk to her at the cemetery, so Carella asked Mrs. Lowery if they might speak to Patricia now. Mrs. Lowery left the kitchen to get her. Sitting at the kitchen table, Carella and Kling could hear voices whispering in the other room. They felt curiously removed from the tragedy that had shaken this house, and yet intimately involved in it. They sat listening.

When Patricia came into the room, her face was tear-streaked. They expressed their sympathies to her, as they had to her mother, and then Carella put a manila envelope on the kitchen table and unwound the string from the cardboard button on the tie flap. He pulled the knife out by the tag attached to its handle and placed it on the kitchen table in front of Patricia.

"Have you ever seen this before?" he asked her.

"Yes," she said.

"Where?"

"It's the knife that killed Muriel," Patricia said. "It's the knife the murderer used."

They went to see Paul Gaddis because there were some things they wanted to know about his party guests. They did not expect to learn what they learned there, and they probably *wouldn't* have learned it if Gaddis hadn't suddenly become hungry. Gaddis was a good-looking young man who'd obviously begun lifting weights at an early age, and who'd just as obviously quit before he'd turned into a musclebound clod. He was sinewy and lean, with a firm, almost overpowering handshake, and an eager, helpful expression on his face. He led the detectives into the living room, and they sat there talking in the golden afternoon light. On Carella's lap was the manila envelope with the tagged murder weapon inside it.

"We want to know who was here at the party," Carella said.

"Not *all* the guests," Kling said.

"Just the ones who were strangers to Patricia."

"Guys she didn't know, you mean?" Gaddis asked.

"Yes," Carella said.

They were, in all honesty, clutching at straws. Muriel Stark had been murdered on Saturday night, and the case was now almost four days old. A homicide case usually begins to cool after the first twenty-four hours. If you haven't got a lead by then, chances are the case won't be solved except by accident. (Pick up a guy accused of rape sometime next Christmas, and during the course of the questioning he'd tell you that back in September he knocked off a little girl in an abandoned tenement on Harding.) This particular homicide looked more difficult than most because it was the result of random violence. Two girls trying to make their way home through the rain. They stop for shelter in an abandoned tenement, and are suddenly facing a man with a knife. Pure chance. So how do you solve a chance homicide except by getting a few lucky breaks of your own? Thus far, their breaks had been limited to the accidental finding of the murder weapon, but the knife told them nothing they hadn't already known. They were here now to explore a possibility that would eliminate chance and give them at least *some* hope of pursuing the case along lines of logical deduction.

"Guys she didn't know, huh?" Gaddis said. "Okay, now that would break itself down into two categories. There'd be guys she didn't know at the *beginning* of the night, but who she might have met before she *left* the party; and there'd be guys she *never* got to meet at all. So which ones do you want?"

"We want anybody Patricia might have classified as a perfect stranger."

"Well, that'd be somebody, say, who came in after she got here, and who hung around in the kitchen with the guys, drinking beer maybe, and who never got to meet her."

"Yes," Carella said. "But who might have *seen* her."

"Mmm," Gaddis said. "Are you thinking that somebody who was here at the party . . . ?"

"It's simply an angle we're considering," Kling said.

"Because we haven't got much else to go on," Carella said honestly.

"Yeah. Well, the thing is, I don't want to get anybody in trouble by saying . . ."

"You won't be getting anybody in trouble."

"Because, you know, my own *father* was here the night of the party, and *he* never got to meet Patricia, though he probably saw her on the way to the kitchen or the bathroom or something, so that would make him one of the guys you're talking about, am I right?"

"Well," Kling said, and looked at Carella.

"Well, *did* your father happen to leave the apartment shortly after Patricia and Muriel did?"

"Not to my knowledge."

"Then that would let him out," Carella said.

"Then what you want," Gaddis said, "is the names of any guys who *didn't* get to meet Patricia, and who also left early."

"Let's start with the ones who didn't get to meet her."

"I think Jackie Hogan got here about a quarter past ten, and I'm pretty sure he didn't meet her. And there was a guy who got here earlier than that, I didn't even know him, he'd come here with one of the girls. I don't think Patricia ever got to meet him because this girl just dragged him in the bedroom and was necking in there with him all night long. But he may have got a look at Patricia, because he came up for air once and went out in the kitchen for a beer."

"What's his name?"

"I don't know his name, the girl never introduced him to anybody."

"Well, what's *her* name?"

"Sally Hoyt."

"Okay, can you think of anyone else?"

"That's about it, I think. No, wait a minute, there was this fellow came in with Charlie Cavalca, he's an instructor of Charlie's down at Ramsey U. Charlie had been downtown in the library, doing some work, and he'd seen the instructor there and told him he was going to a party, so the instructor asked if he could crash. He's a young guy, he teaches English down there. So Charlie called me and asked if he could bring him along, and they picked up two girls in the library and brought them along too."

"Sounds like it was a big party," Kling said.

"There were about fifty people here."

"Your eighteenth birthday party, huh?"

"Yes, but most of my friends are older than that. I run with an older crowd, I don't know what it is. I always did. I'm going with a girl who's twenty-four, for example. My mother can't understand it."

"But Patricia Lowery's only fifteen."

"Yeah, but I wouldn't have invited her, I'll tell you the truth, if it hadn't been for Andy. *He's* my friend, not Patricia. I asked him to come to the party, and he said he wanted to bring his cousin and his sister, so what could I tell him? Could I say no? So I said okay, and then what happens is that he can't make the damn party, so the two girls come alone. I didn't mind Muriel, but you know, lots of the guys were kidding me about Patricia, about having jail bait here."

"Muriel was only seventeen," Carella said.

"I didn't realize that. She looked older. For that matter, Patricia looks older too. But she's kind of immature, if you know what I mean. After all, fifteen is fifteen, no matter how you slice it. The party was big enough to absorb them both, though, so what the hell. I'm only sorry Andy didn't get to come. I'm sure if he'd been here, the whole thing wouldn't have happened later."

"What time *did* he get here?"

"Just after the girls left."

"And he left immediately, huh? To go look for them?"

"Yeah. But then he came back again because it was raining so hard, you see, he figured they might have changed their minds and run back here. But they hadn't. So he left again."

"About these other people you mentioned . . ."

"Right," Gaddis said. "We can eliminate my father, right? Because he never left the apartment all night long." Gaddis smiled suddenly and infectiously. "Besides, he's a very nonviolent type, believe me."

"Okay, let's eliminate your father," Carella said, and returned the smile.

"And I think we can eliminate Sally Hoyt's boy friend, because first of all, she didn't let him out of her sight all night long, and secondly, by the time she got through with him the poor bastard was probably too weak to walk."

"Okay."

"So that leaves . . . Listen, is anybody hungry? I'm starved. Would anybody like a sandwich?"

"No, thank you," Carella said.

"You mind if I make myself one?"

"Not at all."

"Come on in the kitchen," Gaddis said, and rose, and continued talking as they started out of the room. "That would leave Jackie Hogan, who got here about fifteen minutes before the girls left, and who I'm sure didn't get to meet them. And it would also leave this English instructor Charlie Cavalca brought with him. Trouble is, Jackie didn't leave the party till way past midnight, so that lets him out, am I right?"

"That's right."

They were in the kitchen now. Gaddis opened the refrigerator, took out a slab of butter, a loaf of unsliced rye bread, and some ham wrapped in waxed paper. "So that leaves only the English instructor," he said, and turned toward the detectives and smiled again, and said, "Personally, I wouldn't put *anything* past English instructors, but this guy seemed very straight, and besides, he was with a gorgeous blonde he'd have to have been out of his mind to leave." Gaddis walked to the cutting board and reached for one of the knives on the rack above it.

Both Kling and Carella saw the knives on the rack at the same moment. There was a bread knife with a nine-inch-long blade, which Paul pulled down from the rack now. There was also a carving knife with a ten-inch-long blade, and a chef's knife with a six-inch-long blade. But their attention was caught by the paring knives which hung in a row on the rack. There were three of them. They all had wooden handles with stainless-steel rivets in them. They all had blades that appeared to be about four inches long.

"Those knives," Carella said.

Paul Gaddis looked up from where he was slicing the rye bread.

"On the rack there," Carella said. "The paring knives."

"Yeah," Gaddis said, and nodded.

"Were they here on the night of the party?"

"Oh yeah, been here *forever*, those knives."

"Are any of them missing?"

"What do you mean?"

"Should there be *four* paring knives instead of three?"

"Well, there *are* four," Gaddis said, and looked at the rack.

"No, there are only three up there," Carella said.

"There're supposed to be four," Gaddis said.

"Would one of them be in the dishwasher?"

"We never put those knives in the dishwasher,"

Gaddis said. "They've got wooden handles, we wash them by hand. Those are expensive knives. They're made in Germany, you know."

"Would this be the fourth knife?" Carella asked, and opened the manila envelope again, and pulled the knife out by the evidence tag, and put it down on the cutting board. Gaddis looked at the knife.

"Is that . . . is that the murder weapon?" he asked.

"Yes," Carella said.

"It *looks* like one of our knives," Gaddis said, "but I can't tell for sure. I mean, I suppose there are lots of knives that are similar to these. I mean, these aren't unique knives or anything, you can buy them in any good store in the city. But if I had to say, just looking at the knife there, I would have to say yes, it looks as if it could be the fourth knife, it looks as if it could be the fourth paring knife in the set there." He looked up suddenly. "That means he was here, doesn't it?" he said. "The one who killed her. If he took that knife from the rack, he was here."

"Yes," Carella said. "He was here."

Five

At six o'clock that Wednesday night, just as they were preparing to leave the squadroom, the phone on Carella's desk rang. He picked up the receiver and said, "Eighty-seventh Squad, Carella."

"Steve, this is Dave Murchison on the desk."

"Yes, Dave."

"Patricia Lowery here to see you."

"Send her right up."

Carella put the receiver back onto the cradle and turned to Kling, who was rolling down his shirt sleeves. "Bert," he said, "Patricia Lowery's on her way up."

"What does she want?" Kling asked.

"I don't know."

Patricia was wearing blue jeans, a gray Shetland sweater, brown low-heeled walking shoes, and a striped muffler which she had wrapped around her neck so that the ends trailed down her back. The temperature outside had dropped a bit since morning, and her cheeks were glowing and pink. She greeted both detectives by name and then took a seat at Carella's desk. The first thing she said was, "I want to make a statement."

"What about?" Carella asked.

"The murder," Patricia said. "I want to tell you who killed my cousin Muriel."

The detectives glanced at each other in surprise. Neither of them said anything. They waited. Her bandaged hands were in her lap. She sat unmoving in the straight-backed chair, and when finally she began speaking, her voice was almost a whisper, a pained and halting monotone.

"My brother killed her," she said.

Again the detectives looked at each other.

"Yes," Patricia said, and nodded. "My brother."

"Patricia, do . . . ?"

"My brother killed her."

"That's a very serious accusation," Kling said. "Are you sure . . . ?"

"Patricia, do you know what you're saying?" Carella asked.

"I know what I'm saying. My brother killed her."

"On the night of the murder, you told us . . ."

"I was lying. My brother killed her."

"Patricia, I want to tape this," Carella said. "Is that all right with you?"

"Yes. Tape it. I want you to have a record."

Carella went to one of the metal filing cabinets, opened a drawer in it, and pulled out a tape recorder, which he brought immediately to the desk. On the face of the recorder, someone had pasted a label that read PROPERTY OF 87TH SQUAD—DO NOT REMOVE FROM THIS OFFICE!!!! He placed the microphone on the desk in front of Patricia, and then said, "All right, Patricia, you can begin talking now."

PATRICIA: Is it on?
CARELLA: Yes, it's on. Would you repeat what you said just a moment ago?
PATRICIA: I said my brother killed her.
CARELLA: Your brother killed Muriel Stark?
PATRICIA: Yes. My brother killed Muriel Stark.
CARELLA: Okay, just a second, Patricia, I want to make sure we're getting this.

He rewound the tape, played back the segment they had just recorded, and then said, "Okay, we're fine. I'm going to turn this on again, and I want you to tell us exactly what happened. Are you ready, Patricia?"

CARELLA: We're talking now about the night of September sixth. Tell us what happened on that night, Patricia.
PATRICIA: We were at the party. You know about the party, I already told you about the party.
CARELLA: Tell us again, Patricia. *Who* was at the party?
PATRICIA: Muriel and I.
CARELLA: Was your brother there as well?
PATRICIA: No. He wasn't there. He was working. I *thought* he was working. But it turned out he got through early and came looking for us.
CARELLA: All right, you and your cousin were at this party. Is this the birthday party that took place in Paul Gaddis's apartment?
PATRICIA: Yes, it was Paul's eighteenth birthday party.
CARELLA: What time did you get there, Patricia?
PATRICIA: At about eight.
CARELLA: And what time did you leave?
PATRICIA: At ten-thirty. We were supposed to be home by eleven.
CARELLA: Were you and your cousin alone?
PATRICIA: Yes. We left the party alone.
CARELLA: Go ahead, Patricia.
PATRICIA: It began raining again. It had let up a little, but it started pouring cats and dogs again, so we ran up Harding Avenue to Sixteenth Street, where all the stores are. We were standing under an awning there when he came up to us.
CARELLA: Who?
PATRICIA: My brother, Andrew Lowery, my brother.
CARELLA: Came up to you where you were standing under the awning?
PATRICIA: Yes.

CARELLA: Patricia, this isn't what you told us on the night of the murder. When we talked to you then . . .

PATRICIA: I know. I was lying. I was trying to protect my brother. But I realize now that he did a terrible thing, and . . . and no matter how much I love him, I've got to . . . to tell the truth.

CARELLA: All right, Patricia, you were standing under the awning . . .

PATRICIA: Yes, and Andy came up to us, he just came running through the rain, we were so surprised to see him. He said Hi, girls, I've been looking all over for you, or something like that, I can't remember what he said exactly, but it was something like that. And he told us he'd got through work early and went over to Paul's house to pick us up, but we'd already left. So he'd gone downstairs to look for us, and when it began pouring again he went back to Paul's, but we still weren't there, so he came looking for us again, and now he'd found us. I'm just giving you the gist of what he said, those aren't the exact words.

CARELLA: What time was this, Patricia?

PATRICIA: When he found us? Oh, I can't be sure, I guess it must've been about ten to eleven. Maybe five to eleven.

CARELLA: All right, what happened then?

PATRICIA: The rain let up, and we began walking down Harding again, toward Fourteenth, where the construction site is.

CARELLA: The *three* of you?

PATRICIA: Yes. Muriel, my brother, and me. By the time we got to Fourteenth, it started raining very hard again, so we ran into the hallway of this abandoned tenement. To get out of the rain. We were only three or four blocks from home. And we weren't worried about getting home late, because now Andy was with us, we knew my mother wouldn't raise a fuss. Because he could protect us, you see. So we were in the hallway there, looking out at the rain, and I remember I said we should just make a run for it, and Muriel said No, she didn't want to ruin her dress, and Andy said Why don't you take the dress off, Mure? We both thought he was kidding, you know, I mean . . . well, I don't know what *Muriel* was thinking, but *I* certainly thought he was kidding. I mean, Muriel was our cousin, you know? So you don't go around saying things like that to your own cousin—you know, about taking off her dress. You just don't say something, well, *sexy*, like that to your own cousin.

CARELLA: How did Muriel react to his suggestion?

PATRICIA: She said Oh, come on, Andy. Something like that. To just tell him he shouldn't be *saying* something like that, but at the same time not to hurt his feelings. Because they *were* very close, you know, everybody said they were just like brother and sister.

CARELLA: What happened then?

PATRICIA: He said . . . it's really hard to believe this. I still can't believe this was my brother saying these things, or . . . or doing what he . . .

CARELLA: All right, Patricia.

PATRICIA: I'm sorry.

CARELLA: That's all right, take your time.

PATRICIA: I'm sorry, forgive me.

KLING: Here, use one of these.

PATRICIA: Thank you. It's . . . it's just, you see, I expected him to laugh or something, but instead he said I'm not kidding, Mure, take off your dress. And when I turned to look at him, he was holding the knife in his hand.

CARELLA: You hadn't seen the knife before then?

PATRICIA: No. He must've had it in his pants pocket or something. Or maybe in his belt. I don't know. He just pulled it out and there it was in his hand.

CARELLA: The knife you identified for us earlier today?

PATRICIA: Yes.

CARELLA: Is this the knife, Patricia?

PATRICIA: Yes. That's the knife Andy pulled out.

CARELLA: And he told Muriel he wasn't kidding.

PATRICIA: Yes. About taking off her dress, he meant. He meant he wasn't kidding about telling her to take off the dress.

CARELLA: What happened then?

PATRICIA: Well, Muriel, I guess she . . . I'm not sure about this, but I think she giggled. And he . . . he pushed the knife at her, and . . . and grabbed her by the wrist and she started to scream and he told her to shut up. Then, still holding her by the wrist, he forced her down on her knees and said . . . said things to her.

CARELLA: What things?

PATRICIA: He told her to . . . to . . . He was holding the knife on her. He said Go on, take it, I know you want it. I was watching them, I didn't know what to do or say, I just kept watching them. I was so shocked, you see. They were cousins. He was making his own *cousin* do this, his own cousin. It was still pouring. I could hear the rain outside and Muriel grunting, or moaning, on her knees there, with his . . . with the knife . . . with . . . with . . .

CARELLA: Okay, Patricia.

PATRICIA: I'm sorry.

CARELLA: Okay now.

PATRICIA: Then he . . . he started sticking the knife in her. He started stabbing her all over, I couldn't . . . this was my brother doing this . . . my brother . . . I couldn't . . . and then he turned to me, and he said All right, honey, you're next, something like that, and I said Andy, you're crazy, and he said Get down on your knees, and I said Andy, I'm your sister, and he said So what, you're going to . . I can't say it. I'm sorry, I can't say it.

CARELLA: That's all right.

PATRICIA: Do I have to say it?

CARELLA: Not if you don't want to.

PATRICIA: He said . . . oh my God, I can't believe it, I still can't believe he said this to me . . . he said I was going to . . . I would have to . . . I would have to . . . to do what Muriel had done, and . . . I can't say it, I'm sorry. I can't use the words he used.

CARELLA: All right, Patricia.

PATRICIA: And then he began stabbing me. He slashed me on the hands and on the face, he just kept slashing with the knife, and I must have kicked him, I really don't remember, but he was on the floor moaning, so I know I must've done something, and I ran away from him. I could only think he had lost his mind. I could only think my brother had gone crazy. I didn't tell you any of this before because I . . . I still love him, you see, he's my brother. But he's got to pay for what he did, I know he's got to pay. When I saw him at the funeral this morning, and he jumped on the coffin that way, I knew he had everybody fooled, saying he loved Muriel, beating his chest that way and yelling so everybody could hear, Muriel, wake up, say you're not dead, whatever it is he was yelling there, I love you, Muriel, I love you. No, I had to tell you everything I knew, I had to make sure he got punished, the way Muriel was punished.

It was 8:07 P.M.

They had picked up Andrew Lowery at twenty minutes to seven, and now he sat in the squadroom with Detectives Carella and Kling, and Detective-Lieutenant Peter Byrnes, and an assistant district attorney named Roger Locke, and an attorney named Gerrold Harris, who was representing the nineteen-year-old boy. A police stenographer sat on Lowery's left, waiting to record for posterity anything he or any of the others said tonight. Gerrold Harris had spoken to Lowery earlier, and then had told the police and the assistant D.A. that his client would waive his privilege to remain silent, and would voluntarily answer whatever questions they cared to ask him. It was the assistant D.A. who conducted the interrogation. He had talked to Carella and Kling and then had read the transcript of Patricia Lowery's *first* account of the murder, and had listened to the tape she'd made just a little while ago. He sat on the edge of Carella's desk now, and looked at Lowery, and said, "My name is Roger Locke, I'm from the district attorney's office. Your attorney tells me you've waived your privilege to remain silent and wish to answer whatever questions we may put to you. Is that correct?"

"That's correct, sir."

"Are you aware of what your sister has told the police?"

"Yes, sir, I'm aware of it."

"What do you think of her statement?"

"Sir, I think she must have lost her mind, sir. Everything she said was a lie. I didn't even *see* her and Muriel on the night . . ."

"Your sister claims you caught up with them on the corner of Harding and Sixteenth . . ."

"That's a lie."

"She claims she and Muriel were standing under an awning . . ."

"No, sir."

". . . and you came running up . . ."

"No, sir, that's a lie."

"We'll, I'd like to finish my sentence, if I may."

"You can finish it," Lowery said, "but I'm telling you right now that I didn't kill my cousin. I *loved* my cousin, and whatever Patricia told you . . ."

"Well, Mr. Lowery, if you're going to answer my questions, as you've agreed to do, then I'd appreciate it if you'd allow me to phrase them before you . . ."

"I don't think you can blame the boy for interrupting," Harris said. "He's innocent of any crime, and his sister has made an accusation that . . ."

"Counselor, really, this isn't necessary at this stage, is it?" Locke asked. "Your client has agreed to answer our questions, so why not allow me to ask them? Either that, or advise him to remain silent, and we'll all go home, and save ourselves a lot of time."

"All of us but the boy," Harris said. "*He's* not about to go home, is he? He's been charged with homicide, Mr. Locke, and that's pretty serious, I think you'll agree that's pretty serious. So, if you don't mind, whereas I *want* him to answer all your questions, I want his answers in the record, at the same time I wish you'd understand that he's amazed by his sister's accusation, and frankly outraged by it. I do not feel that's too strong a word to describe his reaction. Outraged. So . . ."

"All I'm suggesting," Locke said, "is that I be permitted to put my questions to him."

"Go ahead and put your questions," Harris said.

"Thank you. Mr. Lowery, your sister claims that she and your cousin were standing under an awning on Sixteenth and Harding when you came upon them on the night of September sixth. She further claims that the three of you walked to Fourteenth and Harding, where you took shelter from the rain in an abandoned tenement . . ."

"None of that is true," Lowery said.

"I *still* haven't phrased the question," Locke said.

"Mr. Locke," Harris said, "if you're about to premise your question on something my client states at the top is false . . ."

"Mr. Harris, perhaps *you'd* prefer asking him the question."

"Thank you, no, Mr. Locke. But my client maintains he was *not* with Patricia Lowery and Muriel Stark on the night of the murder. It's pointless, therefore, to ask him questions about anything that allegedly happened in their presence. If you wish to confine your questioning to where my client was at such and such a time, that's another story. But to state as fact something that . . ."

"Let me just *try* a question, may I?" Locke said. "If your client doesn't care for the question, you can advise him not to answer it. How does that sound, Mr. Harris?"

"Let's hear the question."

Locke drew a deep breath, and then said, "Mr. Lowery, did you find your sister and your cousin under an awning at Harding and Sixteenth at approximately ten minutes to eleven P.M. on Saturday, September sixth?"

"I did not," Lowery said.

"Where were you at that time? Do you remember where you were?"

"I was looking for them."

"Where were you looking for them?"

"In the street."

"You had previously been to Paul Gaddis's apartment, is that right? You'd been looking for them there."

"That's right."

"What time did you get there?"

"Paul's place? It must've been about twenty-five to eleven."

"How long did you stay there?"

"Just a few minutes. Just long enough to find out the girls had left. Then I went out looking for them. And it started raining very hard, so I went back up to Paul's, thinking maybe they'd changed their mind. Because of the rain. Because it was raining so hard. But they weren't there, so I went out looking for them again."

"And did you find them on Harding and Sixteenth?"

"No, sir. I never *did* find them. When I got home, my mother told me they weren't there yet, and I said she'd better call the police. Which she did."

"Why'd you suggest that she call the police?"

"Because they'd left Paul's at ten-thirty, and here it was past midnight, and they still weren't home. I was afraid something might have happened to them."

"Did you have any *reason* to believe something might have happened to them?"

"Only that they'd been out in the street for almost two hours, and they still weren't home."

"And you'd been searching for them all that time, is that correct?"

"Not *all* that time. A few minutes of it, I was up at Paul's."

"But we can say roughly, can't we, that from eleven-forty or thereabout . . ."

"Yes."

". . . to a quarter past midnight, you were actively searching for your sister and your cousin. Except for those few minutes when you went back to Paul Gaddis's apartment."

"Yes, you could say that."

"We could say that you'd been searching in the rain for about ninety minutes. An hour and a half, is that right? You'd been searching . . ."

"Yes, that's right."

"Where did you search?"

"Everywhere."

"By everywhere, would you say your search included the corner of Harding and Sixteenth?"

"Yes, sir, I went past Harding and Sixteenth."

"Did you see the girls there?"

"No, sir."

"What time would you say you went past Harding and Sixteenth?"

"It must've been close to eleven. Either a little before eleven or a little after."

"Well, your sister claims that she and your cousin were standing under an awning at Harding and Sixteenth at about ten to eleven, or five to eleven, she wasn't exactly certain. But you've just told me you passed that corner at a little before eleven, and you didn't see anyone standing there."

"No, sir. If my sister was on that corner with Muriel, I must've just missed them."

"I see. And when you continued your search for them, did you happen to wander past Harding and Fourteenth?"

"Yes, sir, I did."

"Past the construction site there?"

"Yes, sir."

"The abandoned tenement there? Did you pass the abandoned tenement?"

"Yes, sir, I did."

"But you didn't see Muriel or your sister."

"No, sir, I didn't see either one of them."

"What time would you say this was? When you walked past the abandoned tenement on Harding and Fourteenth?"

"I couldn't say, sir. I know I got back to Paul's at about a quarter past eleven, so it had to have been before that."

"Before a quarter past eleven."

"Yes, sir."

"And then you went up to Paul's . . ."

"Yes, I went up to see if the girls had gone back there, but they hadn't. So I went down looking for them again."

"And did you go past the abandoned tenement again?"

"No, sir. I went in the opposite direction this time. I began searching in the opposite direction."

"Mr. Lowery, when you were in Paul Gaddis's

apartment . . . You were in there twice on the night of the murder, were you not?"

"Yes, sir, twice."

"Did you go into the kitchen on either of those occasions?"

"Yes, I was in the kitchen both times."

"Both times."

"Yes, I was talking to Paul in the kitchen."

"Did you notice any knives on a rack above the counter top?"

"No, sir, I did not."

"There's a cutting board, from what I understand, that forms one section of the counter top, and above that there's a knife rack. You didn't see that rack?"

"No, sir, I did not see a knife rack."

"Do you recognize this knife?" Locke asked, and shook the knife out of the manila envelope and onto the desk top.

"No, sir, I don't recognize that knife," Lowery said.

"Never saw it before?"

"Never."

"Your sister says it's the knife that killed Muriel Stark."

"I couldn't tell you about that, sir."

"Because you've never seen this knife before, is that right?"

"That's right."

"But your sister *did* see it."

"Then I suppose she knows what it looks like."

"Do you suppose she also knows what the killer looks like?"

"If she says I'm the killer, then she's crazy. That's all there is to it," Lowery said. "She's just crazy."

"You weren't in that hallway with them, is that it?"

"That's it, sir."

"You didn't force your cousin to perform an unnatural . . ."

"Sir, I loved my cousin and I did not kill her. I

simply did not kill her. My sister has got to be crazy, that's all there is to it."

"Do you and your sister get along well?" Locke asked.

"Yes, sir, we do. I always thought we got along fine. But now I don't know what to say, I honestly don't know what's got into her. Sir, if I may make a suggestion, I would like to suggest that you have a psychiatrist look at her, because, sir, she has got to be crazy to be making this kind of an accusation."

"Mr. Lowery, I'm going to ask you some personal questions," Locke said. "If you don't want to answer them, just say so, all right? Is that all right with you, Counselor?"

"Yes, that's fine," Harris said. "I want the record to show that my client has cooperated in every respect. He had nothing to do with this crime, and . . ."

"Mr. Lowery, where do you live, can you tell me that?"

"I live at 1604 St. John's Road."

"With your parents?"

"Yes."

"And your sister?"

"Yes."

"And your cousin, when she was alive?"

"Yes."

"How large an apartment is it?"

"There are five rooms counting the kitchen."

"What are those rooms, can you tell me?"

"There's the kitchen, and the living room, and three bedrooms."

"How many bathrooms are there?"

"Two."

"Mr. Lowery, can you describe the layout of those bedrooms to me?"

"Layout? What do you mean? The way they're furnished?"

"No. The relationship of one bedroom to another. Where they *are* in the apartment."

"What's the point of this, Counselor?" Harris asked suddenly.

"If I may . . ."

"I just want to know what the point is."

"He knows where the bedrooms are, doesn't he?"

"I suppose so, but why . . . ?"

"Will he answer the question or not?" Locke said. "It seems like a very simple question, but if you feel it's in some way incriminating, then please let the record show that your client refuses to answer it."

"He'll answer the question," Harris said. "Go ahead, please. Answer his question."

"Well, the bedrooms are all in a hallway off the living room. My parents' bedroom's on the right, and mine is in the middle, and at the end of the hall the bedroom there is Patricia's and . . . and Muriel's, when she was alive."

"Doors on all these bedrooms?"

"What?"

"Doors?"

"Yes, sure. Doors? Sure, there are doors."

"With locks on them?"

"Yes. Well, the lock on my door is busted. But all the doors have locks on them, yes."

"And where are the bathrooms?"

"There's one where you come in. Between the kitchen and the living room. And there's another in the hall outside the bedrooms."

"So to get to the bathroom from any one of the bedrooms, it's necessary to walk into that hallway."

"Yes."

"For either your sister or Muriel to have gone to the bathroom in the middle of the night, they would have had to walk into the hallway, is that right?"

"Yes, that's right."

"Did that in fact ever happen?"

"What, sir? Did *what* happen?"

"That either of the two walked into that hallway in the middle of the night? To go to the bathroom?"

"Well, I suppose so. I mean, it's perfectly natural for people to get up at night and . . ."

"Yes, but *did* your sister or Muriel in fact ever do so?"

"Yes, I suppose so."

"You saw them in that hallway?"

"I suppose I saw them."

"Your door was open?"

"Sometimes I sleep with the door open. In the summertime, usually. It's cooler that way."

"What were the girls wearing on those occasions when they were in that hallway in the middle of the night? Were they wearing nightgowns? Or were they in fact wearing *any* . . . ?"

"I think that's enough, Counselor," Harris said.

"I was merely . . ." Locke started.

"Yes, I *know* what you were merely," Harris said. "And I am merely telling you that my client will not answer any further questions. Gentlemen, I believe we're finished with the interrogation. Let's get on with what you have to do."

It was now five minutes to nine. In the days before Miranda-Escobedo, cops involved in a big homicide case would try to keep a defendant at the station house long enough to avoid night court. Nine P.M. was usually a safe hour. If the interrogation and the booking and the mugging and the printing went past nine P.M., the prisoner would have to stay at the station house overnight and would not be arraigned till the next morning. Since Miranda-Escobedo, the police were required to begin their questioning as soon after arrest as possible, and were not permitted to keep a man in custody for more than a reasonable amount of time before booking him. "Soon after arrest" and "reasonable amount of time" were not euphemisms. The police respected Miranda-Escobedo because they did not want airtight cases kicked out of court on technicalities of questioning or custody. So these days, even publicity-seeking cops could not delay an interrogation or a booking in order to hit the morning papers with news of having cracked a homicide.

The interrogation of Andrew Lowery was completed by five minutes to nine, but they still weren't through with him. While the assistant district attorney smoked a cigarette and philosophized to Carella about the nicest-seeming kids turning out to be the most vicious killers, Kling took three sets of Lowery's fingerprints, one for the Federal Bureau of Investigation, another for the state's Bureau of Criminal Identification, and a third for the city's Identification Section. As he took the prints, he chatted with Lowery, putting him at ease—the same way an internist will chat with a patient while simultaneously peering through a sigmoidoscope. He told Lowery that in this city a defendant in a murder case was never allowed bail, and he also explained that unless a material witness agreed to be fingerprinted, he wouldn't be allowed bail in *any* kind of case. He wiped Lowery's hands when the fingerprinting was done, and then asked if he would mind having his picture taken. Lowery asked if they wouldn't be taking it anyway when he got to jail, and Kling said Yes, they'd be taking his picture in the morning, but the squad liked to have a record, too, though Lowery could say no if he wanted to. Lowery agreed to have his picture taken, and Kling took a Polaroid photo of him. Then he filled out two arrest cards, and turned the prisoner over to Carella, who had originally caught the squeal, and who was responsible for booking Lowery now.

Together with Lowery's attorney, and the assistant district attorney, Carella and the prisoner went down to the muster room. By that time an assistant deputy inspector had been sent over from Headquarters—this was a homicide arrest—and was waiting at the muster desk. The desk sergeant asked Lowery his name and address, which he wrote into the book, and then he looked up at the clock and wrote down the time and the date, and asked Carella if this was his case. Carella said it was his case, and the desk sergeant wrote his name into the book, too, and then asked him what the case number was, and Carella said it was 12-1430B, and the sergeant wrote that into the book as well. Then, after all of this, he wrote the words "Arrested and charged with (1) Homicide and (2) First-Degree Assault in that the defendant did commit the crimes aforesaid." And he listed as being present at the booking—in addition to Detective 2nd/Grade Stephen Louis Carella—Assistant District Attorney Roger M. Locke, and Assistant Deputy Inspector Michael Lonergan, and attorney for the defendant, Gerrold R. Harris. In the upper right-hand corner of the page, he wrote the arrest number, and then he asked Lowery to empty his pockets, and he made a list of all of Lowery's personal property, and tagged the stuff, and put it into an envelope. In the book, he wrote "And to cell," and then he summoned a patrolman to take Lowery down to the basement, where the precinct's eight holding cells—four for men, four for women—were located. The cells were small, scrupulously clean, each fitted with a toilet bowl and sink, and furnished with a bed and blanket. Locke watched Lowery as he was led out of the muster room. He had not been in handcuffs during the interrogation, but he was in handcuffs now. Several moments later a light on a panel behind the muster desk flashed red, telling the sergeant that one of the holding-cell doors was open. In another moment the light winked out. Locke lit another cigarette. Exhaling the smoke, he said to Carella that this one looked like real meat.

Real meat or not, at eight o'clock the next morning Andrew Lowery was taken by police van to the Headquarters building downtown on High Street, where he was photographed again—this time with a number on his chest—and where the lieutenant assigned checked the fingerprint record that had been forwarded from the Identification Section. The fingerprints were on a mimeographed yellow form, and had been copied by the I.S. from the originals Kling had sent down the night before. Andrew Lowery had never had one before, but he now possessed what the police called a "yellow sheet" or a "B-sheet," and it would follow him for the rest of his life. It followed him to the Criminal Courts Building now, where his name was entered in yet another book before he was turned over to the Department of Corrections. At 9:45 A.M. both Stephen Louis Carella and Gerrold R. Harris were waiting in the Complaint Room of Felony Court when Andrew Lowery was brought in. A clerk drew up a short-form complaint listing the charges against Lowery, and some ten minutes later he was in court with two dozen other defendants, all of whom were waiting to be arraigned. The bridge—the court attendant sitting in front of the judge's bench—read off a defendant's name and the charge against him, and the judge disposed of the case and then the bridge read off another name and another charge. It took quite a while to get to Lowery, because the names were being read in alphabetical order. When Lowery's name was finally called, he stepped up to the bench, and Harris and Carella joined him there immediately. The bridge read off the charges and asked Carella if they were correct as read. Carella said that they were. The judge then said to Lowery exactly what he had said to the ten or twelve defendants who'd been called before him.

"You may have a hearing in this court, or an adjournment for the purpose of obtaining a lawyer or witnesses, or you may waive that hearing and let the case go to a grand jury. Do you have a lawyer?"

"I am representing the defendant, your Honor," Harris said.

"How does the defendant plead?" the judge asked.

"Not guilty," Lowery said.

"The defendant pleads not guilty, your Honor," Harris said, "and requests that the case be held over for a grand jury."

"Very well," the judge said. "The defendant will be held without bail in the House of Corrections until such time as the Homicide Bureau of the district attorney's office shall prepare and submit its case to the grand jury."

And that was it.

Six

Cops know crime statistics.

Which is why hardly anything surprises a cop. Shocks him, yes. He is capable of being shocked. Surprised, rarely. Not where it concerns crime. Carella was shocked when he saw the torn and mutilated body of Muriel Stark in the hallway on Fourteenth and Harding, but he was not surprised that a knife had been the murder weapon. He was not surprised because he knew that forty percent of the annual murders in this city were caused by the use of knives or other sharp instruments, whereas only twenty-seven percent were caused by the use of firearms. He suspected this was due to the city's stringent gun laws; in the United States as a whole, a staggering fifty-four percent of all murders were committed with firearms, the most lethal weapon used in assaults to kill, seven times more deadly than all other weapons combined. Despite whatever the National Rifle Association had to say about man's inherent right to bear arms and to go romping in the woods in search of game, Carella (and every *other* cop in the city) would have liked nothing better than a law forbidding private citizens to own or carry a gun of any kind for any purpose whatever. But police officers did not have a powerful lobby in Washington, even though they were the ones who daily reaped the whirlwind while the gun manufacturers reaped the profits.

Statistics.

It shocked Carella, too, that Andrew Lowery had most probably killed his own cousin. It shocked Carella, but it did not surprise him, because he knew that whereas twenty percent of all homicides stemmed from lovers' quarrels, an overwhelming *thirty* percent resulted from family conflicts of one sort or another. In real life, you rarely got anyone planning a brilliant murder for months and months, and then executing it in painstaking detail. What you got instead was your brother-in-law hitting you over the head with a beer bottle because he was losing at poker. Your brilliant murders were for television, where the smart cop always tripped up the dumb crook who thought the *cop* was dumb but who was really dumb *himself*, heh-heh. Bullshit. Carella always turned off the television set whenever a cop show came on. He sometimes wondered if doctors turned off the set when a doctor show came on. Or lawyers. Or forest rangers. Or private eyes. Carella didn't know any private eyes. He knew a lot of cops, though, and hardly any of them behaved the way television cops did. But a lot of them watched television cop shows. Probably gave them ideas on how to deal with the good guys and the bad guys. Television cop shoves a pistol at a thief, tells him, "This ain't a pastrami on rye, sonny," gives the real-life cop an idea. Next time the real-life cop makes an arrest, he remembers what the television cop said. So he shoves his piece at the thief, and he says, "This ain't a pastrami on rye, sonny," and the thief hits the real-life cop on the ear with a lead pipe and rams the pistol down his throat and makes him eat it, proving if it's not a pastrami on rye, it's at least a baloney on whole wheat with mayonnaise. Television cops were dangerous. They made real-life cops feel like heroes instead of hard-working slobs.

Carella did not feel like a hero when he got back from the Criminal Courts Building that afternoon. He had left the downtown area at eleven forty-five, and it was now almost twelve-thirty, and he still hadn't had lunch, and the first thing he saw on his desk when he walked into the squadroom was a memo from the Police Commissioner. The memo may not have disturbed Carella had he not just been thinking about life imitating art imitating life and so on. But it disturbed him now. It very definitely disturbed him. This is what the memo read:

ATTENTION ALL UNITS, BY ORDER
OF THE COMMISSIONER

1] EFFECTIVE THIS DATE, RUBBER STAMP SIGNATURES MAY NOT BE USED ON ANY OFFICIAL CORRESPONDENCE.

2] EFFECTIVE THIS DATE, ANY ORDERS OR INSTRUCTIONS SIGNED WITH A RUBBER STAMP SIGNATURE ARE TO BE IGNORED.

The memo was signed by the Police Commissioner, Alfred James Dougherty. There was only one trouble with the memo. In signing it, the commissioner, or his secretary, or one of his aides had used a rubber stamp.

Carella looked at the memo and at the rubber stamp signature.

The commissioner had clearly ordered that effective this date rubber stamp signatures could not be used on any official correspondence. The memo also stated that any orders or instructions signed with a rubber stamp signature were to be ignored.

Carella's perplexity was monumental.

He sat at his desk and read the memo again, and then he read it a third time, and tried to decide what he should do about it. His deductive reasoning went something like this:

(1) The commissioner's memo had been signed with a rubber stamp.
(2) Therefore, the commissioner's memo was to be ignored.
(3) If the memo was to be ignored, then the use of a rubber stamp signature on official correspondence was still permitted.
(4) And if the rubber stamp signature was still permitted, then any orders or instructions signed with such a signature were *not* to be ignored.
(5) Therefore, the commissioner's memo was *not* to be ignored.
(6) But if the commissioner's memo was not to be ignored, then it outlawed all rubber stamp signatures, and since the memo had been signed with a rubber stamp, it clearly *was* to be ignored.
(7) Therefore, the commissioner's memo *was* to be ignored and was also *not* to be ignored.

Carella blinked, and looked up at the clock. Only two minutes had passed since the commissioner started causing him heartburn. He decided to go out to lunch.

Until the moment Patricia Lowery made her accusatory statement to the police, they had been looking for a stranger. They were now working directly for the district attorney's office, and looking for evidence to bolster the case against Andrew Lowery. No one doubted in the slightest that the grand jury would, on the basis of Patricia's statement, indict her brother Andrew. In this city a grand jury consisted of twenty-three men, and their purpose was to hear evidence, determine whether a crime or crimes had in fact been committed, whether it was reasonable to assume that the defendant had committed the crime or crimes, and exactly what the nature and extent of the crimes were, for the purposes of indictment. If and when they indicted, the Bureau of Indictment would then make out a list of charges, and two days after that the case would be set for General Sessions, Part I, where the defendant would be arraigned for pleading. The plea in a homicide case was an automatic plea of Not Guilty. At that hearing, clerks from the D.A.'s office would assign the case to a particular judge and a particular part of General Sessions, and a date for the trial would be set. The case against Andrew Lowery was a strong one, even without additional evidence; a sister accusing her own brother of murder was hardly something to be taken lightly. But the D.A. would be grateful nonetheless for whatever else the police could come up with before the case went before a jury. It was for this reason that Carella had tried to get a search warrant while he was downtown at the Criminal Courts Building that morning.

A search warrant is an order in writing, in the name of the people, signed by a magistrate, directed to a peace officer, commanding him to search for personal property and to bring it before the magistrate. The warrant is usually quite specific. The peace officer requesting the warrant must show probable cause and must support this by affidavit, naming or describing the person and particularly describing the property, and the place to be searched. A detective, for example, after being duly sworn and deposed, would state in writing that he had information based upon his personal knowledge and belief and/or facts disclosed to him that an armed robbery had been committed, and then would disclose the results of his investigation before requesting that he be granted permission to search for a suspect revolver which he now believed was hidden in the bread box of the man arrested for the crime.

Neither Carella nor Assistant D.A. Locke felt they had the slightest chance of getting a warrant allowing them to search Andrew Lowery's room in the apartment on Fourteenth Street and St. John's Road. But hope springs eternal, and besides, Carella was downtown anyway, so he took a whack at it, boldly stating in his affidavit that there was probable cause to believe that if there existed in Andrew Lowery's room any clothes bearing bloodstains of the O group or of the A group, then these might constitute evidence of the crime of murder. The magistrate had read the affidavit, and then had fixed Carella with a baleful eye and asked point-blank, "What do you mean by *if?* Do you have any personal knowledge of the existence of such clothing?" Carella had been forced to admit that No, your Honor, he had no personal knowledge of the existence of such evidence, but it was reasonable to assume that perhaps Andrew Lowery—and the magistrate had interrupted to say he was denying the warrant on the grounds that Carella was about to conduct a fishing expedition that would clearly constitute an illegal search. So Carella had gone back to the squadroom, disappointed but not surprised, only to find the Commissioner's baffling memo on his desk.

After lunch he went over to the Lowery apartment *without* a search warrant. The situation here was an interesting one in that the victim and the accused had both lived in the same apartment, and whereas Carella would have needed a warrant to conduct a search of Lowery's room, he did *not* need a warrant to search Muriel Stark's room—no more than he would have needed a warrant, for example, to look for bloodstains or a murder weapon at the scene of a crime. Lillian Lowery opened the door for him, and when he told her why he was there, she asked him to come in. He had been in this apartment before, on the day of Muriel's funeral, but on that occasion he had been concerned solely with positive identification of the murder weapon. He was here today in search of evidence, and he looked at the place differently now, his trained observer's eye automatically summarizing and editorializing.

The apartment was in a fairly decent neighborhood, not quite as good as Silvermine Oval, and nowhere near as elegant as Smoke Rise, but certainly not bad for the 87th Precinct. You wouldn't find any buildings with doormen on St. John's Road, but neither would you find a row of broken mailboxes or hallways stinking of urine. Nor was the Lowery apartment the sort of railroad flat you found in the ghetto sections of the precinct, one room leading directly into another, without benefit of corridor, rather like a string of boxcars following behind a locomotive. Instead, the apartment was arranged like a nest of different-sized boxes, the entrance hall serving as a small receiving chamber off of which one entered the kitchen on the right and living room on the left. The kitchen was a dead-end room, leading nowhere, its two windows opening on the rear brick wall of the building opposite. Curtains on the windows, white nylon sheer; not quite lace-curtain Irish, the Lowerys, nor were they shanty, either. A door directly opposite the entrance door led to what Carella supposed was the bathroom Andrew Lowery had mentioned the night before. In the living room on the left of the entrance foyer, there was a three-piece suite—sofa and two large easy chairs—upholstered in a floral-patterned fabric. Television set against the far wall, framed picture of Jesus above it: one of those trick pictures where the eyes followed you all around the room. Television set was a color console, Carella noticed. On another wall, a picture of a farmer looking up at the sky, possibly hoping for rain.

Mrs. Lowery sat on the sofa under this picture and asked Carella if he'd care for something to drink. He wondered now if she'd been drinking before his arrival. He had not smelled whiskey on her breath, but she'd knocked back three fast ones in a row on the day of the funeral, and he suspected it did not take much to encourage her. She was, and he had not noticed this before, a woman who could be considered attractive, with her daughter's dark-brown eyes and black hair, an abundance of hip and bosom, a rather sensuous mouth. Her eyes were red-rimmed; he guessed she'd been crying. He did not want to chat with her, the afternoon was getting on. But she had already poured herself a shot glass full of whiskey, and had put the bottle down on the coffee table in front of the sofa, and she urged Carella again to have a drink. When he refused, she downed her own drink with one quick toss and swiftly poured herself another.

"I can't believe any of this," she said. Her voice, he now realized, was whiskey-seared—the lady *was* a drinker, funerals or not. He glanced swiftly at her legs, and saw the black-and-blue marks on her shins, the habitual marks of a drunk who bangs into furniture. "Not *any* of it," she said. "First that Andy could *do* something like this, and then that his sister would tell the police about it. I simply . . . It's a nightmare. I woke up last night, I thought it had gone away. I sat up in bed, I thought Dear God, it was all a bad dream, it's gone away. But it was still there, I realized it was still there, my son had killed his own cousin, my daughter had seen him do it, she had *seen* him. Oh my God, it was still there." Mrs. Lowery lifted the second drink to her lips, tilted the glass, and drained it. As she began talking again, she poured herself a third drink. "Can you have any idea how I feel?" she asked. "I loved that girl like my own daughter, I loved her. But how can I believe Andy did a thing like this? And yet I know Patricia doesn't lie, she's not a liar that girl, I know what it must have taken for her to go to the police. I love them *all,* do you see? I'm *caught* in this thing, I love them all. And one of them is dead, and the other one did it, and the third one saw him, oh my God . . ." She lifted the shot glass, drank half the whiskey in it, and then put it down on the tabletop. "May I talk openly with you?" she asked.

"Yes, certainly," Carella said.

"I know you're here to gather evidence against Andy, I know that. I also know that the strongest evidence against him is Patricia's identification. I know that, too. But . . . can you realize how difficult this . . . this *other* thing is to . . . to accept? The . . . the idea of the sex? That he . . . that he forced Muriel to . . . to . . ." Mrs. Lowery shook her head. "And then wanted his own *sister* to . . ." She shook her head again, violently this time, as though the motion would dislodge whatever filthy pictures she had conjured. "This is . . . my *son*," she said. "I haven't even *begun* to think of him as a man yet, he's still a boy in my mind. And now I'm being asked to think of him not only as a man but as some sort of . . . of perverted . . . per . . . per . . ."

She suddenly put her hands over her face, and began weeping into them. Carella sat watching her, not knowing quite what to say. It was, after all, the same old story, wasn't it? The quiet neighborhood boy setting fire to his dear old grandmother and lopping off his sister's head with a meat cleaver. Always had a cheerful word for me, the next-door neighbor would say. Hard-working lad, the grocer who'd employed him would say. Bright and alert in class, never caused any problems, his teacher would say. Sang beautifully in choir, the minister would say. But *also* forced his cousin to commit sodomy, and then brutally stabbed her to death, and turned the same knife upon his sister. What could you say to a woman who had just discovered her only son was a monster?

He waited.

"I suppose you hear this all the time," she said, as though reading his mind. "But I keep trying to remember, I keep looking for clues, anything that would indicate he was . . . was *capable* of this, could *do* this, do you know what I mean? You see, I never once suspected he . . . he was harboring . . . was . . . was . . . May I speak frankly?"

"Yes, please."

"I wouldn't have cared," Mrs. Lowery said suddenly, and lifted the shot glass, and drained it. "I mean, what the hell *difference* does it make? So they were cousins, so what? Haven't cousins fallen in love before, even married before? I'm not suggesting there was even the slightest . . . but even if there was, so what? Would that have been any worse than . . . than *wanting* her so desperately he . . . he had to, to force, to . . . to . . . to do what he finally did . . . to take her by force and kill her? What's wrong with this world, Mr. Carella? I tell you, I swear on my eyes, I tell you I wouldn't have cared *what* the two of them were doing, if only it hadn't come to this. If only it hadn't come to the knife."

Carella said nothing.

"You're thinking, I know what you're thinking. You're thinking what about the sister? He also tried to . . . he also made demands on the sister. Oh my God, I don't know *what* to think any more. I wish I were dead. I wish the ceiling would fall in on me, I wish I would die, please, dear God, let me die, how can I possibly *live* through this?"

She began to weep again, and he watched her and still said nothing, and at last the tears were spent, and she rose and dried her eyes and said, "You wanted to see Muriel's room."

"Please," Carella said.

She took the bottle from the table, carried it to the cabinet from which she'd taken it earlier, put it on a shelf, and then closed the cabinet door. "Andy's room is just across the hall," she said. "Did you want to see that, too?"

"I'm not permitted to," Carella said.

"What's to stop you?" she asked wearily.

"The law," he said.

She turned to look at him. Her eyebrows went up a trifle. She seemed in that moment to be taking his measure anew. Then she turned away and went out into the corridor, and walked directly past the door opening into her son's room. As Carella went past the room behind her, he saw a portion of a bed covered with a blue spread; a wingback chair; a maple dresser against the wall, a mirror over it; a maroon pennant on the wall, gold lettering spelling out HADLEY H.S.

"My bedroom is on the other side of Andy's," Mrs. Lowery said. "The girls' room is here at this end of the hall." She opened a door and stepped aside to let him enter.

It was September on the street, but in that room it was April. Green shag rug and white lacquered dressers. Ruffled bedspreads in yellow and green, curtains running rampant with daisies. A full-length mirror in a white lacquered frame. A desk just under the windows, white formica top, white legs, three drawers. On its top, a yellow lacquered tray for papers, and a lamp with a frosted white globe. Greens in subtly shifting shades, yellows that roamed the spectrum, and a constant white that unified the color scheme. Together they gave to the room the quick bold look of springtime—or of youth.

"This side of the room is Patricia's, here by the windows," Mrs. Lowery said. "Everything on this side of the room is hers. The other side was Muriel's. The girls shared a closet, it's the walk-in closet here by the door, the left-hand side of it was Muriel's, the right-hand side is Patricia's." She hesitated, and then said, "Will you need me? I feel suddenly exhausted."

"I won't take too long," Carella said.

"Mr. Carella?"

"Yes?"

"He couldn't have done it."

"Mrs. Lowery . . ."

"But she saw him, didn't she?"

"Yes, Mrs. Lowery."

"His own sister saw him."

"Yes."

"Still . . ." she said, and seemed to debate the rest silently—tiny shakes of her head, small shrugs, and finally a sigh of defeat. She turned and went out of the room, and Carella heard her shuffling to her own bedroom at the other end of the hall. A door opened and then closed. A key turned, a lock clicked shut.

There were two distinct personalities in this room. He had never seen Muriel Stark alive, had known her only as a corpse on the floor of a tenement hallway, the ceiling above her about to burst from a water leak that had swollen it to grotesque proportions. But she was here in this room as certainly as was Patricia Lowery, and the contrast between the two girls was as palpable as their possessions.

In Patricia Lowery, there seemed to be much of the child.

Full-color photographs of Robert Redford and Paul Newman covered the wall behind her bed, but at the same time—though surely she had outgrown them long ago—a collection of dolls sat like rag-and-plastic siblings on the shelves above and to either side of her dresser. The dresser top itself was neatly arranged with collections of shells, bottles, glass animals, scraps of brightly colored cloth, oddly shaped pieces of driftwood. She had stapled last year's Christmas cards onto a strip of pink ribbon, and had hung this from the ceiling like a mobile; it twisted gently now in the faint breeze that came through the partially opened window. On another ribbon she had similarly stapled picture postcards, and these hung above the full-length mirror. The mirror was lined with photographs tucked into the lacquered white frame, pictures of girls mostly, probably classmates, one of Muriel making a face at the camera, another of her brother Andrew standing on his head and grinning.

In the desk drawers Carella found her stationery (pink with P.L. in the left-hand corner, in delicate script lettering) and an address book, and school notebooks, and an assorted collection of letters she'd been saving for years, some of them addressed to her in Bunk 11 at a camp called Bilvic in Arlington, Vermont. The postmark on the envelopes told Carella she'd been at the camp five years ago, when she was ten. The letters were all from her parents or her brother Andrew. And in those same drawers were compositions Patricia had written in the sixth grade (*How to Train a Turtle* was the title of one of them) and arithmetic tests from God knew how long ago (she was apparently very good in math—all of the tests were graded in the high 90's) and some poems he guessed were recent, judging from the greater sophistication of the handwriting. A look at the paperback novels on one of the shelves told him that her taste in fiction ran to Gothics, or books about nurses, or in one instance (an obvious regression), a book about a little girl and her horse. The magazines she read were *Seventeen* and *Mad*. The calendar on her side of the room was a Charlie Brown calendar, and her piggy bank was a replica of Snoopy. Her records were rock. Hard rock, acid rock, shlock rock —but strictly rock. The clothes in her dresser drawers and on her side of the closet reflected a taste that was somewhat uncertain, somewhat experimental, sometimes babyish, sometimes outrageously sexy; her clothes, in short, were the clothes of a fifteen-year-old moving uneasily toward womanhood.

Muriel Stark, at seventeen, seemed to have got there already.

Where Patricia still clung to a childhood that was slipping away—the various collections, the correspondence, the school compositions and exams, even last year's Christmas cards—Muriel already seemed to have thought of herself as a woman. The lack of any souvenirs may have been due to the fact that she'd lost her parents in an automobile crash two years ago and had come to live in someone else's house; presumably, you didn't carry a trunkful of seashells with you when you were accepting someone's hospitality. But in contrast to Patricia's dresser top, Muriel's was strictly utilitarian, a place for her to put her perfumes and cosmetics, her nail polishes and her jewelry. There was a good light on the dresser, and a mirror over it, and Carella assumed this was where she applied her make-up after having washed in the hall bathroom. A floral-design paperweight was on the far end of the dresser, and it rested on a sheaf of articles clipped from various magazines, each of them describing various career possibilities for women. She seemed particularly interested in becoming an airline stewardess. In addition to several articles on flying, there were two brochures from two different airlines, explaining their requirements, training programs, salaries, and opportunities. The books on her shelves ran mostly to nonfiction, and reflected an interest in a wide variety of subjects. The magazines she read were *Harper's Bazaar* and *Cosmopolitan,* though on the top shelf of her side of the closet Carella found a copy of *Penthouse*—presumably an excursion into the forbidden and not part of her normal reading diet. The clothes on her side of the closet clearly expressed an already developed, sophisticated taste. Her record collection (she presumably had shared the record player with her cousin) consisted only of LP's. There were some albums by rock groups, but she seemed to have outgrown these and was moving more into original Broadway show albums and albums by female vocalists—judging from the preponderance of such material on her shelf. One album seemed to have been played countless times; the sleeve was ragged and the disc inside was worn and scratched. This was Carly Simon's *No Secrets.*

In the top drawer of the dresser, buried under a pile of nylon bikini panties, Carella found a dispenser for birth-control pills. There were twenty-eight slots in the dispenser. The outside ring showed Carella that the last pill Muriel had removed was from the slot marked SAT. She had been killed on September 6, and September 6 had been a Saturday. There was one pill left in the dispenser.

In the hallway outside, Carella heard footsteps.

The door to the room next door—Andrew's room—clicked shut. He listened. He could hear the squeak of the bedsprings in the next room as someone's weight collapsed onto the bed. In a little while he heard someone weeping, the sound clearly penetrating the thin wall that separated the two rooms. He went into the corridor outside, and knocked on Andrew's door.

"Mrs. Lowery?" he said.

"Yes?"

"I'll be going now," he said.

"All right, fine," she said.

"Mrs. Lowery?"

"Yes?"

"Mrs. Lowery, I wouldn't drink any more this

afternoon, if I were you. It's not going to help, Mrs. Lowery." He listened. "Mrs. Lowery?"

"Yes?"

"Did you hear me?"

"Yes," she said. "I heard you."

In the lobby of the building downstairs, Carella took out his notebook and was leafing through the pages when he heard an argument at curbside. A uniformed cop was yelling to the superintendent about having put out his garbage cans too early. The super maintained that the garbage trucks would be here at six-thirty the next morning, and unless he chose to get up at the crack of dawn, he *had* to put them out the night before. Yes, the patrolman agreed, but this *isn't* the night before, this is still the after*noon* before, this is still only two-thirty the after*noon* before. And you've got these dozens of garbage cans lined up at the curb here, stinking up the neighborhood to high heaven, and that's a violation sure as I'm standing here. The super explained that he'd been doing it this way for years now, rolling the garbage cans up from the basement at two-thirty, three o'clock, and he'd never had any complaints from the cop who *used* to have this beat. And he sure as hell hoped nobody was looking for a payoff because he wasn't the type of man to go paying off anybody who was supposed to be doing a damn job for the city. The uniformed cop asked the super if he was insinuating that somebody was on the take, and the super said all he knew was that he was always allowed to roll his garbage cans out at two-thirty, three o'clock, and now all of a sudden it was a big violation. The cop told him it wasn't such a big violation, it was in fact a *small* violation, but it was a violation nonetheless unless he chose to wheel those cans right back down to the basement again, where they wouldn't stink up the whole neighborhood to high heaven. The super spit on the sidewalk, two inches in front of the cop's polished black shoes, and then he spit again and said *that* was probably a violation, too. But he rolled the cans brimming with refuse back down the ramp into the basement. In the morning the Department of Sanitation would find the cans at the curb again, ready to be emptied into the big clanging garbage truck and driven to an area on the Riverhead shore, near the Cos Corner Bridge, where the garbage would be dumped for land fill. But in the meantime, it would not stink up the whole neighborhood to high heaven.

According to Carella's notes, Muriel Stark had worked as a bookkeeper at the Mercantile Trust on Nestor and Sixth. Carella looked at his watch now. It was indeed a little past two-thirty. He'd have to hurry if he wanted to get to the bank before closing.

Seven

He was not looking for trouble.

Patricia Lowery had identified her brother as the killer; the grand jury would undoubtedly indict; there was an excellent chance for conviction even without further evidence. So Carella was not looking for trouble when he went to the bank. But the man in charge of the bookkeeping department was named Jack Armstrong, and he had brown hair and blue eyes. And Carella could not forget that Patricia Lowery—when she'd been lying to protect her brother—had first said the killer was a man as tall as Carella, with blue eyes and hair that was "either brown or black, but very dark." As he stood opposite Armstrong now and shook hands with him, he was looking directly into the man's blue eyes, and the top of the man's brown-haired head was level with his own. He knew there were possibly 2,365,221 dark-haired, blue-eyed men in this city (Patricia had in fact picked one of them out of a line-up when she was still pursuing her initial lie), but it now seemed extraordinarily coincidental that the man who'd been Muriel Stark's boss *also* happened to have dark hair and blue eyes. So whereas Carella was not looking for trouble, he nonetheless wondered whether Patricia had ever *met* Jack Armstrong, and whether this might have triggered an unconscious association. Why, for example, while she was inventing a killer, hadn't she said his hair was blond and his eyes green; or his hair brown and his eyes brown; or his hair red and his eyes blue? Why dark hair and blue eyes—which Jack Armstrong, Muriel's boss, most definitely had? He also had the name Jack Armstrong, and he immediately explained to Carella that this had caused him no end of embarrassment over the years.

"We're both too young to remember this," he said, "but there used to be a radio show called Jack Armstrong, the All-American Boy. I take a lot of ribbing about it. I'll meet a man in his forties, he'll remember the show and begin singing the theme song the minute I introduce myself. Well, not literally, but I'll always get some comment on it. I'm thirty-four, I grew up mostly on television. But you get some of these older fellows, they can name every radio show that was ever on the air. And Jack Armstrong was one of them, believe me."

They were sitting in Armstrong's office at the rear of the bank. A panel of glass some five feet square was on the wall beside Armstrong's desk, affording him a view of the girls working outside. He was smoking a cigar, which he constantly flicked at an ashtray, even when the ash was short.

"I suppose you're here about the Stark girl," he said.

"Yes."

"A terrible thing. Terrible."

"How well did you know her?" Carella asked.

"Not well at all, I'm afraid. I was only transferred from our Calm's Point branch in August, the beginning of August. We hardly had time to get acquainted. But she seemed like a lovely person."

"Mr. Armstrong, as you may know, a young man named Andrew Lowery has been arrested and charged with the murder. He's her cousin, you may have read that in the newspapers."

"Yes, a terrible shame," Armstrong said.

"His sister's name is Patricia Lowery," Carella

said. "She's the one who's identified him as the killer."

"Yes."

"Had you ever met her?"

"Who?"

"Patricia Lowery."

"No. How would I have met her?"

"Well, Muriel worked here, I thought perhaps her cousin might have come to the bank one day . . ."

"No, I never met her," Armstrong said, and shook his head and flicked his cigar at the ashtray. "I hardly even knew *Muriel*, it's not likely I'd have met her cousin. I don't understand. Is that why you came here? To find out whether or not I knew . . ."

"No, no," Carella said. "Actually, I was interested in talking to some of Muriel's friends here at the bank, people she might have . . ."

"You'd want to talk to Heidi then," Armstrong said. "The Stark girl worked at the desk alongside hers, I'm sure they were friends. That's Heidi Beck, shall I ask her to come in?"

"Please," Carella said.

Armstrong buzzed his secretary and asked her to have Miss Beck come to his office. Some three minutes later a tentative knock sounded on the door, and Armstrong said, "Come in." Heidi Beck was a good-looking blonde in her early twenties. She was wearing form-fitting slacks, and very high platform shoes, and a short-sleeved sweater over a long-sleeved blouse. When Armstrong introduced her to Carella, she seemed relieved that she hadn't been called to the office for a reprimand. Armstrong came from behind the desk, told Carella to take all the time he needed, and then left the office. Through the glass panel on Carella's left, he could see Armstrong working his way through the bookkeeping department, stopping to chat with one or another of the girls at their desks.

"Mr. Armstrong tells me you and Muriel Stark were friends," Carella said.

"Yes," Heidi answered. "Well, I *guess* so. I mean, we weren't *close* friends or anything, but we'd go out to lunch together every now and then. And we'd talk during the day. I guess we were friends as far as the bank goes, do you know what I mean? We never saw each other *away* from the bank, except like I said to have lunch every now and then."

"Did you and Muriel ever discuss personal matters?"

"Well, there was quite a bit of age difference between us," Heidi said.

"How old *are* you, Miss Beck?" Carella said.

"I'm twenty-four. Muriel was only seventeen, you know. So we really didn't talk about too many personal matters."

"Ever talk about boy friends?"

"No. We'd say this or that fellow in the bank was cute, something like that, but we never talked about boys we were going out with, no."

"Did Muriel think any of the boys in the bank were cute?"

"Oh, sure."

"Who in particular?"

"Well, nobody in particular that I can remember. But she had an eye for the boys, she liked boys. In the beginning, anyway."

"What do you mean?"

"When she first started working here."

"When was that?"

"She began in February. And, like I said, she used to, you know, give the boys more of a once-over when she first started. Then, I don't know, she didn't seem too interested any more. I had the feeling she'd found herself a boy friend."

"Did she ever mention a boy friend?"

"No."

"Then what gave you the idea she had one?"

"Well, like I said, fellows would stop at the desk and make a comment to her—she was a very pretty girl, you know, dark hair and really beautiful brown eyes, and a good figure, too—so the fellows would stop to talk to her or, you know, make comments, flirt with her. And in the beginning she used to encourage that a lot, but then it sort of tapered off, she wouldn't pay too much attention."

"When was that? When it began tapering off?"

"Oh, I don't know. April sometime? Yeah, before Easter, I guess it was."

"That she stopped paying attention to the fellows."

"Yeah. Well, I mean she didn't give them the cold shoulder or anything, but you could see she wasn't really interested."

"And you think that's because she found herself a boy friend."

"Yeah, that's what I think. But that's only my opinion. Like I said, she never mentioned having a boy friend or anything. I just put two and two together, that's all."

"What do you mean?"

"Well . . ." Heidi shrugged. "I'm a little embarrassed talking about this."

"Think of me as a priest," Carella said, and smiled.

"I'm Jewish," Heidi said, and smiled back. "Besides, I'd be embarrassed even if you *were* a priest."

"Well, give it a try," Carella said.

"Well, this must've been in August sometime, I don't know exactly when, the beginning of August sometime. Muriel came over to my desk and started hemming and hawing around, and finally asked me if I knew a good gynecologist. Well, I don't know what that means to *you*, but to *me* . . . well, it meant a lot."

"What did it mean to you?"

"Well, she's a seventeen-year-old kid, right, she lives with her aunt, right, so if she's having some sort of problem a gynecologist should look at, why doesn't she ask her *aunt* about it? Instead of coming to a stranger? So I figured it had to be one of two things. I figured either she was pregnant already or else she didn't want to *get* pregnant. You know what I mean?"

"I think so," Carella said.

"I could spell it out for you," Heidi said, "but it embarrasses me."

"Did she say *why* she needed a good gynecologist?"

"She said she had some kind of itch, or . . . God, *listen* to me, will you? You're only a *cop*, I shouldn't be talking to you about such things."

"Muriel was killed," Carella said simply.

Heidi looked into his eyes, nodded, and then flatly and matter-of-factly said, "She was complaining about a vaginal itch, I think it was. Or a discharge, I'm not sure I remember. I gave her the name of my gynecologist and I also mentioned that he'd fitted me for my first diaphragm. In case that was why she wanted to see him. I didn't *suggest* she was seeing him for that reason, but at the back of my mind I figured I'd put her at ease, if that's what she wanted. Or if she wanted to be put on the pill. She was only seventeen, you know, a kid going to a strange gynecologist. But I'll tell you, it was my idea she was pregnant. You know why? I shouldn't have to tell you this, you're a detective, you probably figured it out already. But when she asked me that morning, she didn't just say did I know a gynecologist. She said did I know a *good* gynecologist, you see the difference?"

"Yes," Carella said, and nodded.

"Because a girl who just wants a diaphragm or some pills, she'll go to any *shlepper*, am I right? She'll pick one out of the phone book, what does she care? But Muriel wanted a *good* gynecologist, which meant this was something important, never mind a vaginal itch. I figured she was pregnant." Heidi looked up sharply. "*Was* she pregnant?"

"The autopsy report didn't say anything about it," Carella said. "Normally, they don't look for something like that unless they're specifically asked to."

"It might've been *worth* looking for," Heidi said, and then immediately added, "Look, who am I to tell you how to do your job? I'm probably wrong, anyway. They were very strict with her, you know, so the chances of her being pregnant were probably . . ."

"*Who* was strict with her?"

"Her aunt and uncle. Wouldn't let the poor girl breathe."

"Is that what she told you?"

"No, it's just something else I figured out."

"On what evidence, Heidi?"

"On the evidence that every afternoon he was waiting outside the bank to take her home from work."

"Who? Her uncle?"

"No, her cousin. Andrew Lowery. The one who killed her."

"I took better care of her than I did my own daughter," Frank Lowery said. "No one can fault me for the way I took care of Muriel."

It was three-thirty in the afternoon, the men were sitting in Lowery's auto body shop on Boomer and Third. Outside the small cluttered office, Carella could see workmen restoring fenders and panels. The sharp stench of lacquer and enamel hung on the air, and intermittently the sound of a hammer banging on metal punctuated the conversation.

"Wasn't an easy thing taking a new member into the family," Lowery said. "This was two years ago, I didn't own the shop then, I was struggling to make ends meet as it was. But this was my wife's niece, I didn't figure I could turn her out in the cold, there were no other relatives could take her in. Man has responsibilities, don't he?" Lowery said. "Man loves his wife, he's got to love her kin, too. I'll tell you though, may God forgive me, if I'd known it would come to this, I'd have turned her over to a home, I'd have never taken her in. You try to do the Christian thing, and then . . ." Lowery shook his head.

"Mr. Lowery, what I'm trying to find out is whether there was any indication that something like this might be brewing. Had Muriel and Andrew argued, had they . . . ?"

"Got along beautifully," Lowery said. "Look, they were brother and sister, that's it. You can write that down. They were brother and sister, that's the way I raised them, and that's what they were. Anybody in the family wanted anything, I considered them all like my own kids. Muriel wanted something, same as if Patricia did. Or Andy. They were all my children, that's the way I felt about it from the day I took Muriel in my house. She called me Uncle Frank, that's true, but she could've just as easily called me Dad, because that's what I was to her. And a good father, too, I think. Got her anything she wanted, but I laid down the law, too, that's part of a father's job, ain't it? Laying down the law? Did it for Patricia, *still* do it for her, and did it for Muriel, too."

"Laid down the law in what way?" Carella asked.

"Well, dating for one thing. I *still* won't let Patricia date boys, she's too young for that. Now I know you've got kids nowadays, they're going steady at thirteen, *twelve* some of them, but I won't permit that, no, sir. I wouldn't let Muriel date till she reached her seventeenth birthday, and even then I insisted on meeting every boy she went out with. Had to come to the house to pick her up, had to look me right in the eye, shake hands with me. None of this blowing the horn downstairs, anything like that. And she had a strict curfew, too, had to be home by midnight, not a minute after. Night of the party we made sure they'd be coming home by *eleven* —that's because they were alone, just the two girls. I'd have gone to pick them up, but I was sick that night, a touch of the flu, and it was raining so bad." Lowery paused, looked at his hands. In the shop outside, a cloud of green paint struck the fender of a car like a plague of grasshoppers. "I keep thinking . . . what if I *had* gone to meet them? What if I'd seen my own son . . . my . . . my own son hurting those two girls? Mr. Carella, this is the worst thing that's ever happened to me in my life, ever. If I live to be a thousand, there's nothing can happen to me will ever be worse than this. I've lost Muriel, who I loved like a daughter, and I'll be losing my boy, too —he'll be going to jail for life, I'm sure. And God knows what this whole thing will do to Patricia, what effect it'll have on the girl's mind. She's only fifteen, to have a terrible thing like that happen, seeing what she saw, and then Andy turning on her like a wild animal. Mr. Carella, I don't think any of us will ever be the same again, after this. Ever. I sometimes believe Muriel is the lucky one, at least she's out of it. *We'll* have to live with this for the rest of our lives, and there are times I wonder if I can make it."

"Mr. Lowery, I understand your son used to go down to the bank to meet Muriel after work. Is that true?"

"Yes. That's true. He did."

"Did *you* ask him to do that?"

"No, no. I was protective, yes, but I wasn't a nut on the subject. I mean, a girl coming home from work at five in the afternoon, there's nothing to fear *there*, is there? I know there've been people killed or raped in broad daylight, but you can't live your lives that way, you can't keep hiding in a closet, can you? No, I felt Muriel was perfectly safe coming home from work alone. I guess Andy went down there to get her because they had so much to talk about, you see. He'd been accepted in college, and they were all the time discussing the courses he would take. Never a meal went by in this house without the two of them talking about Andy's college education. He respected that girl a lot, and her opinions, which is why I can't . . . I . . ."

"Would you say it was *his* idea to pick her up after work?" Carella said.

"Well, I don't know. I guess the two of them. I guess it was arranged by the two of them. Andy wasn't doing anything during the summer, so I guess he didn't mind driving downtown to get her, and I guess Muriel was grateful she didn't have to take the train home during the rush hour. I really couldn't say, Mr. Carella. But it wasn't *my* idea, that's for sure, I had no fear for her safety at five in the afternoon. What *did* bother me was when she'd call and say she'd be late, either working late at the bank, or else shopping if it was a Thursday night, that's what got me upset."

"Did she do that often?"

"Well, often enough. I told her about it, I gave her hell about it. I treated that girl like my own daughter, Mr. Carella. I miss her sorely. I truly miss her. I loved that girl. She was a very dear person to me."

"Mr. Lowery, on those occasions when your son picked up Muriel at the bank—did Patricia ever go with him?"

"No, I don't think so."

"Had she ever gone to the bank on her own?"

"Not that I know of."

"Then she wouldn't have known any of Muriel's fellow workers?"

"No."

"Never would have seen any of them."

"That's right."

They were silent for several moments. Outside in the shop, the hammer started again, and Lowery waited till it was silent, and then said, "What causes something like this, can you tell me? Where a kid you think the world of, bright and good-looking and gentle as can be, just suddenly goes crazy and does something like this? What causes it, Mr. Carella?"

"I don't know," Carella said.

"I've been trying to figure it out. Ever since Patricia told us what *really* happened that night, I've been trying to figure what got into Andy. Muriel kept a diary, you know, I went into her room and looked for it, thinking maybe there was something in it that would explain what happened. She kept that thing faithfully, used to write in it every night before going to bed. But I couldn't find it. Don't know what could've happened to it. I looked all through that room for it, it just isn't there."

"Mr. Lowery," Carella said, "would you mind if *I* looked for it?"

"Not at all. It's red leather, I gave it to her for Christmas, in fact. One of those little locks on the front, with a tiny key, do you know the kind I mean?"

"Yes," Carella said. "Thank you, Mr. Lowery, you've been very helpful."

This time he had something specific to look for, and the something was a diary Muriel Stark had kept. Neither he nor Mr. Lowery had found the diary when they'd separately searched her room, and in his affidavit requesting a search warrant, Carella stated that there was now reasonable cause to believe that the accused, Andrew Lowery, might have stolen the diary on the assumption that it contained incriminating evidence. *Wherefore,* Carella petitioned, *I respectfully request that the court issue a warrant and order of seizure in the form annexed authorizing a search of Andrew Lowery's room in Apartment 3A at premises 1604 St. John's Road and directing that if such diary bound in red leather and written in Muriel Stark's hand, or if any part of this diary or evidence in the crime of murder be found, that it be seized and brought before the court, together with such other and further relief that the court may deem proper.*

The warrant was granted.

Carella got back to the Lowery apartment at twenty minutes past six that evening. Frank Lowery was already home from work, and he and his wife were having their dinner in the kitchen. They explained that Patricia had been sent to her grandmother's for a week or so. They had not thought it wise to send her back to school just yet, not while the newspapers were playing the story up so big. They asked Carella if he would care to join them for dinner, and he graciously declined their invitation and then searched their son's room from top to bottom.

He found no trace of the diary.

At 6:45 A.M. the next morning, a Department of Sanitation truck pulled up in front of the building on St. John's Road. One man was driving the truck and two men were walking behind it. The walkers were also lifting garbage cans and tossing the contents onto the conveyor that dumped the refuse into the truck. These men liked to bang garbage cans around; this was evident in the way they smashed the cans against the metal rim around the conveyor, and also in the way they slammed the cans down on the sidewalk again. The average garbage can on any city street got battered and bruised within the space of a week because these men loved their work so much. (Some people insisted these men also loved the smell of garbage, but that was pure conjecture.) What they loved was banging garbage cans around and griping about being sanitation employees. Sanitation employees were always going on strike or contemplating going on strike. That was because they figured their jobs were as dangerous as policemen's or firemen's. Firemen were always complaining that *their* jobs were more dangerous than policemen's, but sanitation employees figured *their* jobs were more dangerous than either of the other two, and therefore they wanted at least the same amount of money for this very dangerous work they did.

"It's dangerous," Henry said, "because first of all the fuckin people don't respect us." Henry was driving the garbage truck. The two men who'd been walking behind the truck were now on the front seat beside him. The truck was full now, the men were heading toward the Cos Corner Bridge, near which they would dump the garbage before continuing with the second leg of their route. A sanitation truck could hold only so much garbage, and once it was full to capacity, the garbage had to be dumped someplace. This was an elementary rule of garbage collection. It was, in fact, the first tenet of the sanitation game: When it's full, empty it. "They don't respect us," Henry said, "because they think of us as garbage men. We are not garbage men. We are sanitation employees."

"Sanit men," George said. George was one of the men who'd been walking behind the truck. He was glad to be on the front seat now, being driven to the stretch of land the city was filling in near the bridge. A man could get tired of walking behind a garbage truck and lifting garbage cans and smacking them gleefully against the rim of the conveyor. He was certainly glad to be sitting for a while. Moss sat alongside him. Moss was the truck's other walker, the only black man on the team. They worked well together, these three, despite their racial differences. They liked to believe, and perhaps it was true, that there was no room for prejudice in the sanitation game.

"That's exactly what we are, George," Henry said. "Sanit men."

"And entitled to respect," Moss said.

"*And* the same damn pay the cops and the firemen get," George said.

"Now *that's* the issue," Henry said. "That's the issue *exactly*. And that's why I think we've got to strike again."

"Do firemen have to handle the waste of an entire city?" George asked.

"All that *shit* they put in the garbage there?" Moss asked.

"Firemen *don't* have to handle that shit," George said, answering himself.

"Neither do policemen," Henry said.

"All that slimy shit," Moss said. "We ought to get paid a *fortune* for handling all that smelly shit."

"But every time we ask the city for a raise, you know who gets on their high horse?" Henry said. "The cops. They get on their high horse because they want the city to think they're the only ones risking their lives on the line out there every day. Well, I ask you, my friends, when's the last time you heard of a cop getting garbage dumped on his head by the superintendent of a building where Murphy's been collecting the garbage there for fifteen *years!* Fifteen *years,* mind you, and the animal who runs that building turns on him. Like an *animal!* Dumps a full can of garbage on his *head!* Murphy *still* stinks from it."

"All that slimy shit," Moss said.

"Should pay us a fortune," George said.

In the distance they could see the slender lines of the Cos Corner Bridge, and to the left the area the city was filling in with refuse. Gulls winged against the September sky, dipping and wheeling over the garbage dump. Down on the flats, there were several other sanitation trucks unloading. Henry cut off the main highway and let the truck roll down the dirt road to the flats. The gulls were shrieking and cawing and making a terrible racket.

"Do cops have to deal with sea gulls?" George asked.

The traffic manager, standing knee-deep in garbage, signaled for Henry to pull the truck over to the left, which he did. The traffic manager then jerked his thumb skyward, signaling Henry to dump the load. Henry pulled a lever inside the truck, and the back of the truck began tilting, and the refuse from some hundred and fifty apartment buildings began tumbling onto the ground, joining the bottles and newspapers and orange rinds and coffee grounds and meat bones and soggy stringbeans and mashed potatoes and empty cartons and old shoes and cigar butts that had been collected from all over the city in the past weeks and months. Included in the garbage that had been collected that very day at 1604 St. John's Road was a diary bound in red leather. The strap holding the diary's clasp to the lock on the cover had been cut.

Fresh garbage kept falling onto it.

Not twelve miles from the Cos Corner Bridge, in another section of Riverhead, Carella was trying to talk an adamant old lady into letting him see her granddaughter. The woman was Matilda Lowery, and she was eighty-four years old, and she insisted that Patricia had had enough to do with policemen. Her parents had sent her here to keep her *away* from reporters and policemen, in fact, and if Carella didn't get away from the door, he would get hit on the head with a broom.

Carella explained that he was working for the district attorney's office, gathering evidence that would help in the prosecution, and there were several questions he wanted to ask Patricia, questions he was certain would be brought up at the trial, when the case finally came to trial. The old lady was seriously raising her broom and seemed ready to crown Carella with it when Patricia called from the other room and said it was all right to let him in. Matilda Lowery shook her head, and went muttering into the kitchen to make herself a pot of tea.

This was still just a little past noon on Friday, September 12. Patricia was wearing blue jeans and a white sweater. Her dark hair was braided into pigtails on either side of her head. She looked much younger than her fifteen years, and seemed quite calm now that the ordeal of accusation was behind her. Her hands were still bandaged, and a piece of adhesive plaster still clung to her right cheek. She asked Carella to sit, and then immediately said, "Do you think I'm doing the right thing? Not going back to school yet?"

"Yes, I think that's the right thing," Carella said.

"I'm not sure. I don't want the kids to think I'm a coward."

"I'm sure they won't think that," Carella said.

"They *already* think I'm a rat," Patricia said.

"What makes you say that?"

"I got some phone calls. Before I came here to Grandma's. And also, I received a letter."

"Have you still got the letter?"

"I threw it away. It frightened me."

"What did it say?"

"Oh, it just called me all sorts of horrible names

for having ratted on my own brother. The phone calls were the same. One man said he would kill me if he ever saw me on the street."

"Well, I wouldn't worry about that happening," Carella said.

"No, I realize a person has to be a little crazy to make a call like that. But . . ."

"Yes?"

"Do you think I did the right thing? Would *you* have done it? If you'd seen your brother committing a crime . . . committing *murder* . . . would you have told on him? Do you have a brother?"

"I have a sister," Carella said.

"Would you have told on her?"

"Yes."

"I keep wondering," Patricia said, and sighed heavily. "Anyway, it's too late, I've already done it. There's no changing anything now." She sighed again, and then said, "What did you want to ask me?"

"Just a few things, Patricia. First, when we talked to you on the night of the murder, you said a dark-haired, blue-eyed man . . ."

"I was lying," Patricia said immediately.

"Yes, I know that. To protect your brother."

"Yes."

"But why'd you pick on that particular combination, Patricia? Dark hair and blue eyes? Was there any reason for that?"

"No. I don't think so."

"Do you know a man named Jack Armstrong?"

"No."

"He was Muriel's boss," Carella said. "He has brown hair and blue eyes."

"I don't know him," Patricia said.

"You see, I might as well tell you this, the identification is going to be challenged," Carella said. "Your brother's attorneys are certainly going to challenge the identification."

"Why? I ought to know my own brother," Patricia said.

"Yes, but you see, Patricia, you were so insistent

about the *first* identification, and it turned out to be a false identification. So the defense is going to try to make something out of that, I'm sure of it. Which is why I wanted to know whether you'd ever met Mr. Armstrong. Because then, you see, in trying to cover up for your brother, you might have unconsciously picked somebody who was in some way connected with Muriel. But you don't know Mr. Armstrong."

"No."

"Your father mentioned that Muriel went out on dates, and the boys came to pick her up at the house. Do you remember any of those boys?"

"Some of them," Patricia said.

"Would any of *them* have had black hair and blue eyes? I'm sorry to keep harping on this, Patricia, but I'm positive the identification will be challenged, and anything we can do to help the district attorney . . ."

"I don't remember what any of those boys looked like," Patricia said. "Some of them only went out with her once or twice. I didn't even know their names, some of them."

"Well, then that's the end of that, I guess," Carella said, and sighed. "There's just one other thing. Your father mentioned that Muriel kept a diary, said she wrote in it faithfully every night. You shared a room with her, did you ever see her writing in a diary?"

"Yes, I did."

"Would you describe it to me?"

"It was red leather, with a little strap that locked onto the front cover."

"When did you last see that diary, Patricia?"

"I guess she was writing in it the night before she was killed."

"Last Friday night?"

"Yes."

"And what did she do with it afterwards?"

"She locked it and put it back in her drawer. She used to carry the key on a chain around her neck."

"Which drawer did she keep it in?"

"The top drawer of her dresser."

"It's not there now, Patricia. Would you have any idea where it might be?"

"No. That's where she always kept it."

"Well," Carella said, and then shrugged. "Okay, I guess that's it. Sorry to have bothered you. Thanks a lot, Patricia."

The man thought of himself as royalty.

He thought of himself as the monarch of all he surveyed. This was *his* city, and as the reigning potentate he was entitled to his daily tithe. He would have sent menials to collect for him, except that he so enjoyed doing it himself. Especially at this time of year. He had been born in September, guessed that had something to do with it. Baby first sees the light of day in a certain season, why, that's *got* to affect the way he feels about life from that minute on. Imagine being born in February or March, coming bare-ass naked into a world so cold, doctor slapping you, drawing that needle-sharp air into your lungs, enough to make even a prince shudder! He loved making the daily rounds in September, when the skies above were invariably blue and the air was like a maiden's kiss. Oh, how they loved him! Oh, the things they put out for him each day, his loving subjects! Oh, the surprises! He never knew what the tithe would be, never could even *hope* to guess what gifts he would find in alleyways or mews, curbside container or back-lot carton.

And today—today he had found a mountain of treasure, he could not believe his eyes at first. It was not yet his birthday, and so the barbarian hordes from beyond the city walls were not required to bring a percentage of their plunder through the gates to lay at his feet. Nor was it yet Christmas, when those of the Christian faith who inhabited the lands to the south and to the west were required to bring to him in measure equal to his weight riches beyond imagination. And yet, here upon the Cos Corner plain, his subjects had strewn for his pleasure a carpet of gifts extending to the very horizon, causing him to widen his jaded old eyes in surprise and smack his toothless gums in delight. In the shadow of the bridge he danced upon the endless treasure trove, plucked a skeletal umbrella from one glittering mound, twirled it over his head, trailed a tattered pink boa on the fragrant breeze, poked and picked for trifles and fancies, tried on a pair of pale-blue gloves and a pendant with a broken stone, and then settled back into an easy chair with its stuffing showing, and in the late-afternoon light began to read a book bound in bright-red leather.

On the front page of the book, he read the printed words:

THIS IS THE DIARY OF

And below that, written by hand on the appropriate blank line:

Muriel Stark

The name sounded familiar, one of his loyal subjects, no doubt—Muriel Stark. Had he read another book about her adventures? Was this a sequel? Muriel Stark. And then he remembered seeing her name in a newspaper he had plucked from a garbage can just a few days ago, and he remembered, too, that she'd been murdered. He got out of the chair and tucked the diary into the pocket of his long black coat. Then, tossing the pink boa back over his shoulder, twirling the stark umbrella over his head, he went looking for a policeman.

Eight

Carella had always believed that anyone who kept a diary did so only because he was hoping it would someday be read by another person. The lock would be picked, the strap would be cut, the pages would be opened, and the diarist would stand revealed to the prying eyes of a stranger. In all the diaries he had read during his years as a cop, he had never come across one in which the diarist seemed unaware of a potential audience. Some diarists plainly acknowledged the possibility of later readership by writing entire pages in code; presumably there were *some* entries they considered fit for broadcast but others they chose to keep secret. The codes were very often so simple, however, that they ceased to be codes at all—further indication that the diarist intended them to be understood all along. It did not take a mastermind, for example, to crack a code that moved each letter one letter forward in the alphabet, so that the world's most famous epithet would appear as GVDL ZPV. Some of the codes were more complicated, but none of them were terribly difficult to decipher. Usually, the pages written in code dealt with specific sex episodes or wild fantasies. Never violence. It was rather strange. If a man committed an act of violenee, the entry would appear in his diary in plain, undisguised English—"Today I broke Charlie's head with a hammer." But if he'd had an unusually heady *sex* experience, then the entry would appear in code—"In Carol's room yesterday, I did DVOOJMJOHVT on her." Dvoojmjohvt was neither Dutch nor Swedish. Nor was it a voodoo curse. It was merely brilliant code, the kind any diarist hoped would be licked in six seconds flat. Such was the way of all diarists. They pretended that the words they committed to the pages of their secret books were sacred and profane, but at the same time they were clearly writing for an audience.

Muriel Stark's diary did nothing to change Carella's mind.

He did not read it in the best of surroundings: a detective squadroom at ten past five on a Friday afternoon is not exactly the reading room of the public library. The diary had been delivered to him via radio motor patrol car direct from the 106th in Riverhead. The Riverhead patrolman to whom Crazy Tom had turned over the diary ("I suggest you take a look at this, my good man," Tom had said) had checked out the first page and had been alert enough to recognize the name of a homicide victim. Suspecting a possible hoax, he had nonetheless given the diary to his sergeant, and the sergeant—also suspecting a hoax—had taken it back to the 106th, where he'd passed it on to the desk officer, who immediately sent it upstairs to the detective squadroom, where a Detective/Third named Di Angelis was at last smart enough not to add his fingerprints to the collection already there. Accepting the diary on a clean white handkerchief, he carried it into his lieutenant's office, and the lieutenant checked out the name on the first page, and then called Homicide and was informed that the case was being handled by a Detective Stephen Louis Carella of the 87th Squad, who could be reached at Frederick 7-8024. The lieutenant from the 106th had called Carella at once, and then had offered to send the diary downtown in a radio motor patrol car. Carella had graciously accepted the offer. Now, wearing white cotton gloves and gingerly turning pages, Carella read Muriel Stark's diary, and became more and more convinced that she (like other diarists he had known) was writing for posterity, each word chiseled on the granite of the page. It was difficult to tell whether Muriel was actually feeling anything at all, or feeling everything with the same unbearable intensity, or simply pretending to feel things for the benefit of her future unseen audience. She used no codes, unless one could consider flowery language or literary allusions codes of a sort. At times her prose was sickeningly sentimental. At other times it was morose and self-pitying. She wrote passionately of womanly yearnings and desires without the slightest indication that she understood either. Even in April, when she fell madly in love and began recording what she referred to as "the single most exciting experience in my life," she seemed thoroughly aware of her phantom reader, and so her lover became a phantom as well, never named, never described except in language so ethereal that it vanished like mist.

"Get your fuckin' hands off me, you cocksucker!"

Carella looked up from the diary. Meyer Meyer was shoving a husky white man toward the detention cage across the room. The man's hands were cuffed behind his back, but he kept trying to butt Meyer with his head as Meyer shoved him along. Meyer would shove at him, and the man would stumble forward a few feet and then turn and lower his head like a goat and try to butt Meyer all over again. As he rushed forward, Meyer would put his hands out to stop the thrust, and then he would spin the man around and give him another shove toward the detention cage. At the cage, Hal Willis was waiting with the door open. There was an amused expression on his face. He was thinking that Meyer would have made a good bullfighter.

"Leave me the fuck *alone!*" the man shouted, and lowered his head again, and started running forward again. This time Meyer didn't shove him. This time he brought the hard edge of his right hand down on the back of the man's neck, and then brought his knee up into his chest. Then he dragged the man over to the cage and pushed him into it, and angrily slammed the door shut.

"You son of a bitch," the man said.

"Shut up!" Meyer said.

"What'd he do?" Willis asked.

"Stuck an icepick in his father's eye," Meyer said, and took out his handkerchief, and wiped his face, and then blew his nose, and glared at the man in the cage.

Carella turned his attention back to the diary.

On a Saturday afternoon in May, Muriel's lover had taken her to a movie, and had kissed her for the first time. She described the kiss as being "sweet as falling rain," and wrote that her "heart stopped dead." Two days later her lover had met her downtown, after work. She explained to the diary again (although this information had appeared in an earlier entry) her reasons for having dropped out of high school. And she explained again, to the diary (or to her spectral audience), just how much she liked her job as a bookkeeper at the bank, and how good it made her feel to be able to contribute money to the house, though Uncle Frank and Aunt Lillian practically had to have the money *forced* upon them, but still they accepted it, and this made her feel good, to know she was independent and self-sufficient. But what made her feel better than anything in the world was knowing that she was loved, knowing that when he touched her she soared "to a sunrise of expectation. How long will it be before he wants from me the ultimate ecstasy? I will give him whatever he wishes," she had written. "I will open myself fully unto him, for he is my love."

The telephone on Kling's desk rang, and Carella looked up. Kling snatched the receiver from its cradle, and said, "Eighty-seventh Squad, Kling. Yeah, just a minute, I've got that right here on my desk someplace. Genero? Can you hold just a minute? Right, hold on. Okay, here it is, have you got a pencil?

We've got a problem here because it could have been fired from two different guns. That's right, Genero. Look, I'm telling you what Ballistics told *me*. You want an argument, call them. Guy I spoke to there is named Firbisher. *Firbisher*. F-I-R-B-I-S-H-E-R. He said the twist was sixteen inches left, and the groove diameter was point four-oh-two inches. Now this is what that means, Genero. That means it could've been either a .38-40 Colt or a .41 Colt, because both those revolvers have the same rate of twist and groove diameters. How can that *be?* What do you *mean*, how can that be? It *is*, that's how it can be. Look, Genero, how do *I* know how he made his tests? Am I a Ballistics expert? He probably put the thing under a microscope, how the hell do I know what he did? You asked me to take a message if he called, and he called, and that's what he told me, and that's what I'm giving you. This is not my case, Genero, this is your case. That's right, it *is* your case, I just *said* that, didn't I? It's your case, yes. *Who's* sticking his nose into it? Genero, you want to know something? You're a pain in the ass, Genero. How you ever got promoted into this squadroom is beyond me. That's right. That's what I said. Right. *Sure*, remember it. I *hope* you remember it. I hope you never *forget* it, Genero. I hope, in fact, you never ask me to do another favor for you, Genero, because you know what I'll say? I'll say no. That's right. That's what I'll say. I'll say no. Now if you don't mind, I've got work to do. Goodbye, Genero."

He slammed the receiver down onto the cradle, muttered, "You no-good bastard," and then realized that Carella—sitting at his own desk not three feet away—was watching him. "Genero," Kling said in explanation, and went back to his typing.

Carella went back to reading Muriel's diary.

The "sunrise of expectation" continued all through the month of May. As Carella waited patiently for Muriel's defloration, the suspense became almost unbearable. He followed the girl's panting declarations of undying love with bated breath, wondering when her anonymous lover would make the move that would at once rob her of her virginity and at the same time satisfy a sunrise that was becoming increasingly more purple as the summer approached. By the end of May, Carella began to think her lover didn't exist at all. Muriel had invented him, he was a figment of her imagination, a true phantom, a character created only to add a little zip to the diary. Or, if he *did* exist, he was certainly a shy and cautious soul whose explorations thus far had been limited to touching her breasts "naked beneath the bra," as she put it. In the first few weeks of June, Muriel began wondering when he would "move below the waist."

Carella, by this time, was hoping the lover would move to Alaska. He kept turning the pages of the diary, though, trapped in a pornographic treatise that lacked not only socially redeeming value but also specific gravity. As Carella read about all the various "aches," "tingles," "throbs," and "tremors" Muriel was feeling above the waist (*and* below), he couldn't help thinking that if only her nameless lover had been treated to a prepublication glimpse of her diary, he'd have leapt upon her in broad daylight and violated her in public, even *if* it frightened the horses. But through most of June her mysterious lover remained blithely unaware that Muriel was longing to be "taken in passionate delight," as she put it, a ripe blossom waiting to be plucked, so to speak. Carella lived through the agonizing details of a stealthy finger-walk up the inside of Muriel's thigh, a trembling hand sliding into her panties to probe at last "the aching mound where my sweet womanhood lies." This was on the twenty-eighth of June, a Saturday. On the Fourth of July, while fireworks exploded overhead (symbolically and cinematically, and perhaps realistically as well), Muriel Stark lost her virginity on a deserted Sands Spit beach. The entry concerning this gala event had been made on July 4, but immediately beneath the printed date on that page, Muriel had written, "*Really* July 5, since it's now 3:00 A.M., and I've just returned from Sands

Spit." There followed a passage describing in detail the steamy adolescent intensity that had led to the sandy seduction anticipated for months by thousands of breathless fans. Reading the diary with a critical eye, Carella had to admit that the big seduction scene was given all the space it required, spilling over from the page allotted to July 4 and onto the pages for NOTES at the back of the diary. Nor had Muriel ever written better. What with the fireworks and all, the big seduction scene was a critical and commercial smash.

And then the tone of the diary changed abruptly.

Where there had been almost daily entries *before* the night of Muriel's defloration, the first entry after the one for July 4 was July 15. Carella kept turning blank pages, vaguely disappointed, wondering if the diary had ended with the big sex scene, and beginning to think again that the whole damn thing had been invented for the dubious pleasure of the reader. When he came to the July 15 entry, he read through it with a rising feeling of disorientation, scarcely able to believe it had been written by the same person who'd written the preceding pages. It was as though he'd been reading a novel (he still could not shake the belief that *none* of this was real) by a writer whose style he'd begun to understand if not particularly admire, and suddenly *another* writer had been brought in to finish the book. The entry was brief, the language plain, the gushing adolescent seemed to have disappeared overnight (or rather in the space of eleven days, the time that had elapsed since the entry of July 4 and the entry of July 15), to be replaced by someone who sounded strangely sober and . . . well, troubled.

He did not know why Muriel suddenly seemed unable to handle what she'd been yearning for since that first kiss in the balcony of a movie house in the merry month of May. He did not know until he read the entry for August 1. It was then that he learned who her lover was, and realized he was *not* a phantom, and understood why she had not named him till now. She had kept the secret until it became impossible to bear, but now she was forced to share it—if only with her diary. On August 1 her diary became her confessor and her confidante, and Carella was certain she locked it from that night forward. And whatever else he had previously believed about Muriel (and all *other* diarists), he changed his mind abruptly when he realized she was now putting down her thoughts only in an attempt to find answers to problems that were suffocating her. The unfortunate thing was that by the time of her last entry on September 5, the night before her murder, she seemed to have found none of the answers she was so desperately seeking.

Friday, August 1

I'm sure I'm pregnant.

Today I told him. I told him I hadn't mentioned it before because I was sure I'd get my period, but now it was almost a week, it was six days to be exact, and I had to tell him. He was very calm about it. He said I shouldn't worry. He said I'd have to see a doctor, take the rabbit test, make sure I *was* really pregnant, and then we'd see what we had to do.

I said Andy what *can* we do? If I'm pregnant, what can we do? We're cousins, Andy. We're first cousins. Dear God, if you're listening, let me get my period.

Saturday, August 2

I love him so much, that's the trouble. But I know it's wrong. We both know it's wrong. We shouldn't have done it, we shouldn't have started it. He said I have to make an appointment with a doctor, but what doctor should I go to? I'm so embarrassed. Should I tell the doctor the truth? Or should I just pretend Andy is some boy I know, and not my cousin?

Monday, August 4

This morning I asked Heidi if she knew a good gynecologist. I told her I was itching and didn't know anybody to go to, and was embarrassed to ask my aunt. Heidi is twenty-four years old, she said she'd been going to this one man, a Dr. Henry Keller, since she was eighteen, in fact got her first diaphragm from him. I called him on my lunch hour, and his nurse told me the first appointment she could give me was for the tenth. I said this was an emergency, and she said What sort of emergency, and I said I think I'm pregnant. Did you want a rabbit test? she asked. Yes, I said, that's what I want. She asked me how late I was, and I said it was nine days now, and she said if I didn't get my period by tomorrow, then on Wednesday I should go directly to a lab for the test. She gave me the name of a lab that did tests, and I thanked her and hung up.

Andy picked me up after work, and I told him I was going to wait another day and then go to a lab. He said okay. We were walking along toward his car. I told him I hoped I wasn't pregnant. I asked him what we would do if I was pregnant. He said we would see.

Tuesday, August 5

I did not get my period, so I called the lab today and made an appointment for tomorrow during my lunch hour.

Andy looks so worried. I'm sure the whole family knows something is going on.

Wednesday, August 6

I'm so happy I could scream! It's only seven o'clock in the morning, but I had to put this down before I start getting dressed for work. Yes, yes, *yes!* Thank you, God! I'm going to knock on Andy's door, and wake him up and tell him. I don't care if everybody in the house hears us. Well, I *do* care. But, oh Jesus, I'm so damn happy!

Thursday, August 7

Andy told me today he was ready to marry me if it turned out I was pregnant. He said there was nothing wrong with cousins getting married, and he was in fact thinking of telling his mother that's what we planned to do. I said I didn't think that was such a good idea, telling his mother, I meant. He said Why not, don't you love me, Mure? I told him I loved him more than life itself. And that's true, that's really true. But I didn't want him to be making any wild promises just because he'd been so scared about my being pregnant. And I also said I was sure there was something wrong with cousins getting married, I was sure there was something in the Bible about it. He asked me where in the Bible? I told him I didn't know exactly where, but I was sure it was in there someplace.

Saturday, August 9

I went to see Dr. Keller today, but not to find out if I'm pregnant, which thank God I'm not. I went to ask him to prescribe birth control pills for me. I did this because from now on, I want to make sure we're absolutely safe. Andy still wants to tell his mother that we love each other and want to get married, but I'm sure I'm right about her going through the ceiling, and also I'm sure Uncle Frank will throw me right out of the house if *he* ever finds out.

Dr. Keller was an old man in his sixties, he prescribed the pills without a fuss, but he also gave me a little lecture about not using them as a license for promiscuity. I told him I was engaged to be married, and he said that was nice to hear and he wished me luck. I told him my period had started on the 6th, and he said I should take the first pill on the 11th, and then keep taking them till all twenty-eight pills were gone. Then I could expect my next period a few days after that, and counting the day I got my period, I should allow five days and then begin taking the pill again the very next day. It sounds very simple.

Thursday, August 14

I didn't realize Andy could be such a jealous person.

I was waiting for him outside the bank today, he must've been about ten minutes late, he explained that he'd got caught in traffic. But I was talking to Mr. Armstrong, who's head of the bookkeeping department, a very nice person who's old enough to be my father, I really mean it. Well, he's at least thirty, anyway, and he's married and has a small daughter. Anyway, we were just standing there talking, passing the time, when Andy pulled up in his car. I said goodbye to Mr. Armstrong, I don't even know his first name, and I got in the car, and the first thing Andy wanted to know was who was that I was talking to. I told him it was a man who worked in the bank, Mr. Armstrong from the bookkeeping department. So Andy wanted to know what we were talking about. I told him I'd been waiting there on the sidewalk, and when Mr. Armstrong came out he saw me standing there and we started chatting, that was all. So Andy *still* wanted to know what we were talking about. I said Why, are you jealous? And he said he would kill me if ever I started up with another man.

I think he meant it.

Saturday, August 16

Today Andy told me his plan.

Everybody was out of the house this afternoon, they all went to the beach—Uncle Frank, and Aunt Lillian, and Patricia. I told them I had shopping to do, that I needed some new clothes for the fall, and Andy lied and said he had a date. So we got to stay home alone. We made love in Andy's bed for the first time. I really feel great now that I'm taking the pill. Andy says it's turned me into a wild animal, whatever that means. Maybe he's right. I just don't worry about a thing now.

His plan sounds stupid to me.

His plan is not to go to college in the fall. After he's been accepted and everything. Instead, he says he wants to work full-time at the steak joint, as a waiter no less. He says he can make plenty of money waiting tables, and he says with both our salaries, we could live very well. In short, he wants to marry me as soon as possible, forget about college, take our own apartment, etc. I told him that's all his mother has to hear. First that he wants to marry his own cousin, and next that he's dropping out of college to do it. Andy says he doesn't give a damn about his mother, but I told him I'd have to give this a lot of thought. He said Why? What's there to think about? We love each other, don't we? I said I loved him dearly, but dropping out of college before he even *started* was really kind of stupid. And besides, I was only seventeen, I wouldn't be eighteen till March, which made me underage. His mother was my guardian and she'd never sign for me to get married. He said the hell with her, we'd elope. I said Andy, let me think about it, okay? Then we made love again before they got home.

I really *do* feel like a wild animal when we make love.

Monday, August 18

Mr. Armstrong stopped me on the way out to lunch today, and asked me if that was my boy friend who picked me up all the time. I said No, it was my cousin. That's really the truth, but of course the other is the truth, too. Andy *is* my boy friend. Mr. Armstrong asked me where I was going, and I said out to lunch, and he said Of course, how stupid of me. Where *else* would you be going at twelve-thirty? He asked if he could walk with me, and I said Sure, Mr. Armstrong, why not, and he said I should please call him Jack, which is his name. He said he'd taken a lot of ribbing about being named Jack Armstrong, but I didn't know what he meant, and he explained that there used to be a radio show, oh, back in the thirties he guessed it was, and the hero of it was Jack Armstrong, the All-American Boy. He said that was before my time. I said that was probably before *his* time, too, wasn't it, and he said Oh, yes, I don't remember it personally, my parents told me about it. He said he was twenty-six years old, which really came as a surprise to me, because honestly he looks much older. Anyway, he dropped me outside the R&R, and I went in for a sandwich, and didn't see him the rest of the afternoon. He really *does* look a lot older than twenty-six.

I didn't mention any of this to Andy because I don't want him to take a fit about nothing.

Sunday, August 24

In church this morning, I prayed to God that Andy would change his mind about going on to college in the fall. Registration is September 8, which is just a little more than two weeks away. Please, dear God, I ask you again. Let him change his mind. We love each other a lot, but telling Aunt Lillian about us now would be the wrong thing to do, I feel. Besides, I think he's rushing things. It's not as if I was pregnant, which I'm not.

Monday, August 25

Jack came over to my desk this morning, and asked if I would like to have lunch with him. The first thing I thought was that Andy would get very angry if he ever heard about it, and then I figured there'd be nothing *really* wrong with it, except of course Jack is married. So I said Well, thanks a lot, Jack, I really appreciate your asking, but you're a married man and all, I happen to know you're married and have a four-year-old daughter. (It was Heidi who'd told me this.) So Jack said What difference does *that* make, all I'm asking is whether you'd like to have lunch with me. I'm not taking you to Singapore for a six-month tour of the Orient. Well, I thought that was pretty comical, and also pretty honest, so I said Sure, why not, let's have lunch together.

He's a very fascinating person.

He's not what you'd call good-looking, but he has a very interesting face with a lot of character in it. His hair is brown, I guess, but so dark it could almost be black. And his eyes are blue, and I suppose he's just about six feet tall, give or take a few inches.

He told me that his father used to be a

coal miner in a place in Pennsylvania, I forget the actual name of the town, but the people there call it Scooptown. And he said he himself had never worked in the mines, that he'd been fortunate enough to get a football scholarship to college, and to get out of Scooptown when he was just eighteen. He met his wife while he was an undergraduate out in Michigan, and then she'd worked for a while to put him through school while he was going for his master's. He started at the bank only four years ago, just a little before his daughter was born, but he expected he'd be promoted to assistant manager before long.

He also told me that he absolutely did not want me to get the wrong idea about us having lunch together. He wasn't on the make, in fact he'd tell his wife all about it, that was how innocent the whole thing was. Besides, he knew I was only seventeen, he certainly wasn't about to rob the cradle. Though I *was* very pretty, he had to admit that. In fact, if his wife asked him tonight, he guessed he'd have to say I was beautiful. He made me blush, I mean it. I mean, I'm *not* beautiful. I'm just not. But it was nice of him to say so.

I told Andy I'd had lunch with him.

I didn't tell him Jack had said I was beautiful.

Andy was very quiet when I told him. He didn't say anything for a long time afterwards. Then later, we were watching television, everyone had gone to bed, and we were sitting in the living room watching Johnny Carson, and out of the blue Andy said You don't really love me any more, do you, Mure?

I told him he was crazy.

He blew his nose then. I think he was crying.

Of *course* I love him.

I adore him, in fact.

Tuesday, August 26

Today I got an answer to the letter I wrote to United Airlines. I hadn't told Andy I'd written to them (and also one other airline) and now he wanted to know why I'd done that behind his back. I told him I hadn't done anything behind his back, and he said that writing to an airline was something behind his back. What did I plan to do? he said. Take a job with an airline? And go flying all over the world? I told him United doesn't fly outside the United States, and he got angry and grabbed my wrist and said I shouldn't kid around when he was being serious. He said I knew *exactly* what he meant, whether it was all over the world or all over the United States didn't make a damn bit of difference. What he meant was that I'd be taking a job where we'd be separated a lot. I told him I wasn't *taking* a job, I hadn't even *applied* for a job, all I'd done was write some letters of inquiry, that was all. Besides, in the material from United, it said I had to be a high-school graduate and at least twenty years old to become a stewardess. I'd dropped *out* of school, and I wasn't eighteen yet, I wouldn't be eighteen till March. So it was a long-range thought, even if I *did* decide to maybe become a stewardess one day. He said that an airline stewardess was nothing but a waitress with wings, did I want to become a goddamn waitress? And that's when I blew up and said to him what did *he* want to become? A waiter in a steak joint?

That's when he told me he planned to register for college, after all. We were in his car, we were parked on a street about six blocks from the house. I turned to look at him, I said Andy, that's wonderful. I'm very happy to hear that, Andy. And he said Sure, I know why you're happy. You're happy because my going to college means we won't be able to get married for a while, that's why you're happy. I told him that getting an education was more important than rushing off to get married, and he said again that I didn't love him any more, he could tell I didn't love him any more.

I don't know what's the matter with him, I mean it.

Wednesday, August 27

In bed tonight, I was reading the Bible. Patricia asked me how come I was suddenly interested in religion. I told her I was only interested in the stories, there were some interesting stories in the Bible. What I was looking for was proof that what Andy and I are doing is wrong. I *know* it's wrong, but I can't find anything in the Bible that says so. Even so, I know that if I'd have been pregnant that time, we could have had idiot children, I know that for a fact. There *has* to be something wrong with it, otherwise you'd see plenty of cousins married to each other, brothers married to sisters even. But a society protects itself by making laws against that sort of thing—though I don't know if there's a *real* law against it. I'm sure there's a religious law, though.

Nine

Carella looked up at this point, puzzled, and then opened the top drawer of his desk. From it he took a paperbound edition of the state's criminal law, and thumbed through the index at the rear till he found the word INCEST, and a referral to page 151. On that page, he found:

Incest

—

PL 255.25

—

Class E
Felony

and alongside that, under the word "Elements,"

> Marrying or engaging in sexual intercourse with a person whom one knows to be related to him, either legitimately or illegitimately, as an ancestor, descendant, brother or sister of either the whole or the half blood, uncle, aunt, nephew, or niece.

No mention of cousins. Whatever the *Bible* had to say about matters incestuous, the Penal Law was clear. If you were kissing cousins, that was quite all right with the state. Carella couldn't quite understand the niceties that made it okay for a boy to marry his cousin whereas that boy's father, who would be the girl's uncle, could *not* marry her unless he wished to be charged with a Class E felony and sent to jail for a maximum of four years. In the eyes of the law, however, Muriel and Andrew hadn't had a thing to worry about. Carella turned back to the entry for August 27.

> But a society protects itself by making laws against that sort of thing—though I don't know if there's a *real* law against it. I'm sure there's a religious law, though. That much I'm sure of.
>
> As I write this now, Patricia is watching me from her own bed across the room. She interrupted me not a minute ago to ask what I can possibly find to write about each night. I told her that a million things happen every day, and I just try to put them down so I won't lose track of them. She told me that all the things that happen to her are just boring, and it would bore her all over again to write them down.
>
> Well, she's really very young. I love her a lot, but she's only fifteen. There's a difference.
>
> Thursday, August 28
>
> Jack took me to lunch again today.
>
> He's really a very mature and level-headed person, different from Andy in so many ways. I can't imagine Jack, for example, taking a fit about a little old diary. This morning I happened to mention to Andy that Patricia had asked about the diary, and he immediately wanted to know if I'd written anything about us in it. I said Yes, I'd written a lot about us. He said I mean about *us*, you know. I said Yes, about *us*, you know. I was smiling when I said this, and imitating his voice a little, and he suddenly slapped me, we were sitting in the kitchen having coffee, he slapped me and the cup of coffee fell on the floor, and Aunt Lillian called from her bedroom, wanting to know what was going on. The walls

in that apartment are paper-thin, you can hear everything all over the house. Andy said there'd been an accident, cup of coffee fell off the table, and Aunt Lillian said to be sure to wipe up the linoleum, and Andy said he would.

Then, while he was wiping the floor, he looked up at me and said there was nothing funny about any of this, he couldn't understand why I'd begun taking it so lightly. I said I didn't think it was funny at all. In fact, *I* was the one who kept saying it was wrong whereas all *he* wanted to do was get into my goddamn *pants* all the time! He told me to shut up, the whole house would hear me, but I really didn't give a damn by then who heard me, I *mean* it. That slap had really hurt. He had no right slapping me that way. I finally told him the diary was none of his damn business, and when he asked me if he could read it, I said absolutely *not.*

The point I'm making is that Jack never would've reacted that way, I'm sure he wouldn't. He's very big on privacy, Jack is, which is one of the reasons his wife drives him up the wall. She can't stand him doing anything without her. He sits down to read a book, his wife comes over, asks him what he's doing. He's sitting there reading a book, right? So she asks him what he's doing. What he usually says is he's riding a camel across the Sahara or he's building an ark for when the rains come—ask a stupid question, you get a stupid answer. But she does that all the time, whenever he's trying to read or listen to some music, or even when he's down in the basement working on something, she'll come over and pester him—What are you doing, Jack? He said it's because she's really quite an empty person inside—vacuous was the word he used, if that's the way you spell it—and whereas he still loved her, there were times when he wished she was more self-sufficient. He told me this in all honesty, and said it wasn't just a "My Wife Doesn't Understand Me" pitch. He hoped I realized he wasn't coming on with me, he just found me very interesting to talk to, and besides, he liked looking at me because I was so damn lovely. Those were his exact words—"so damn lovely." He covered my hand with his when he said this. He put down his fork and covered my hand. I didn't mind it at all. I thought I'd feel embarrassed, his being married and all. Instead, it made me feel good. He's a very nice person, and I'm sorry he's having trouble at home. If some people could just understand that a person doesn't want to be *owned.* Well, I guess it's very hard for some people to understand that.

Friday, August 29

I had to lie to Andy today.

It was such a beautiful afternoon that around three-thirty, four o'clock, Jack said it might be a good idea if we took a drive into the next state at the end of the day, he knew a nice little place over there where we could go for a drink. Andy usually picks me up outside the bank at a little after five, which is quitting time. The bank closes at three, of course, but we stay on till five. I told Jack I didn't know whether or not I could make it because my cousin would be coming down to get me, and he grinned and said he was beginning to wonder about this *cousin* of mine, was I sure this guy was a *cousin?* I said Oh, sure, he's a cousin, all right, and he's supposed to pick me up. So if I can't get him on the phone, well then, we'd have to forget about it, or I'd have to take a raincheck for some other time. I also told Jack that a person had to be twenty-one to drink in *this* state, and they were always asking me for my I.D., but he said I didn't have to worry because it was eighteen over the bridge there, and I certainly looked eighteen and he didn't think anybody would bother me. Well, I called Andy and told him I had to work late, there was a hundred and four dollars we couldn't account for, and we were all going crazy trying to track it down. I told him I'd catch the train home, and he said Okay, he'd see me later. He also said he had some good news for me.

The place Jack took me to was about twelve miles over the Hamilton Bridge, a very nice little cocktail lounge attached to a motel. He was right about nobody asking me for my I.D, though the man who served us *did* look me over very carefully. When I mentioned this to Jack, he said that's because I was so beautiful. He said if a man *didn't* look me over carefully, he had to be crazy. I really get kind of fluttery when he says things like that, I don't know what it is. He told me again today how devoted he is to his wife, though she's been pestering him about taking a vacation before the summer ends. Leave the kid with her mother, go away just the two of them. He told her he didn't think he could get away right now, and suggested that she go alone—but of course she doesn't understand or need privacy. He said he was sort of wishing she'd go. He's a very nice person, I'm really sorry about the situation with his wife.

When I got home, Andy was waiting for me downstairs. He told me he'd gone to see a priest, and he'd asked the priest whether the Catholic church objected to marriage between first cousins. The priest said the church would permit the marriage of persons related to the third degree of kindred, which meant that we would have to be *third* cousins in order to get married with the church's blessing. So I asked Andy why he considered that *good* news, and he said the priest had told him special dispensations were sometimes granted, and that it was possible one might be granted for us. I told Andy it seemed like a lot of trouble to go through, just to get married, and he looked at me very strangely and said he thought the news was going to please me. Then we went upstairs, where supper was waiting, and neither of us said a word all through supper. Aunt Lillian wanted to know if anything was wrong. I told her No, nothing was wrong.

Saturday, August 30

Andy came into my room at ten o'clock this morning. I thought he was crazy at first, but he told me everybody was out of the house. He was wearing only pajama bottoms. I told him he should get out of there before someone came home, and he said he didn't care if they all found out about us, he loved me and wanted to marry me. I told him the priest had said first cousins couldn't get married, and he got very angry and said I hadn't listened to him at all when he'd told me about the special dispensation that was possible. I told him I had listened very carefully, but I was sure dispensations weren't just handed out every day of the week, that it was probably very rare that the church allowed first cousins to get married. He admitted that the priest had told him as much yesterday, and had also added something about it being bad to mix the blood. But he said he honestly didn't give a damn *what* the church thought—who said we had to get married by the church? We could go right downtown and get married at City Hall, what the hell was so special about getting the church's blessing? I said Andy, if it isn't so special to get the church's blessing, then why did you go to see a priest yesterday? Andy, I think it *is* important to you, and it's also important to me. And if the church is so against it, there must be a reason, and we ought to reconsider, maybe we ought to think about it for a while instead of rushing off and doing something we'll regret for the rest of our lives.

He was in bed with me by then, and he was on top of me and trying to get my nightgown off. I told him to please stop, I didn't feel like it right then. He said I used to feel like it all the time, but now I *never* seemed to feel like it, and I said That's right. With you harping at me all the time about getting married, that's *right*, Andy. You're killing any desire I might be feeling, that's absolutely right. He got out of bed and went out of the room, and I heard him getting dressed next door, banging closet doors and dresser drawers, and then I heard him storming out of the house. I didn't see him all day today.

Sunday, August 31

In church this morning, I prayed that God would help me to break off with Andy.

I can't bear it any longer.

I have to be free of him.

He didn't say a word to me all day. At supper tonight, he looked sullen and angry, and finally Uncle Frank told him to please leave the table if he didn't know how to behave with human beings. Andy got up and went straight to his room. I'm sure they're all going to know what's going on if he doesn't quit acting this way. He must think they're all fools.

Monday, September 1

Today is Labor Day, which means the bank is closed and I won't get to see Jack. All this weekend I've been longing to talk to him. I just can't go on this way, I've got to have someone to talk to about this situation. I've been thinking of running away from here, but I know that would hurt Aunt Lillian, and she's a dear sweet woman who I love a lot. If only I hadn't started with Andy. If only I'd been stronger. I have to tell somebody about this.

Tuesday, September 2

The first thing I did when I got to work was call Jack's office. His secretary asked who this was, and I said it was me, and said I thought I'd found a bookkeeping error. When she put Jack on the line, I explained that I needed desperately to talk to him. We agreed on a place to meet for lunch, and at about a quarter to one I began telling him the whole story.

He was shocked.

He said the first thing I had to do was get out of that house. I told him I couldn't do that immediately, I would first have to find a place to stay. He said he'd help me do that, and he warned me that meanwhile I must not have anything to do with my cousin, that the situation could only deteriorate. From what I had told him about the various times Andy had become violent with me, Jack was frankly fearful for my safety. I told him I didn't think there was anything to worry about in that respect, and he said I certainly hope so, Muriel, because if anything should happen to you—and then suddenly he got very quiet, and he looked down at his plate. Finally I said Yes, Jack, what *if* something should happen to me? He said he was sorry he'd said that. He was a married man, and I was only a seventeen-year-old girl, and he had no right to express any interest in me other than what a good and concerned friend might express. So I said Don't you consider yourself something *more* than a good and concerned friend, Jack? And he said All I know is I'm worried about you, Muriel. I want you to get out of that house before your cousin takes it into his head to harm you.

I assured him that Andy wasn't the type who'd *really* hurt me. Even though he'd slapped me that one time, and grabbed my arm a couple of times, I told Jack I didn't think he was really the violent type. Jack said he was worried, anyway, and he suggested that I take a room in a hotel downtown until I could find a place of my own, but I told him my Uncle Frank would never permit that. In fact, I was going to have a hard-enough time of it just moving out. I was only seventeen, after all, and my Uncle Frank and my Aunt Lillian were my guardians. And Jack said If they're your guardians, they should have made certain their goddamned son kept his filthy hands off you.

And that was when I started crying, and he took me in his arms right there in the restaurant and told me not to worry, he would never let anyone or anything harm me.

I'm really frightened in this house now that Jack has succeeded in making me aware of the danger here. Andy is still walking around with a long face, and I know that both my Aunt Lillian and Uncle Frank are wondering what's going on between us. I'm just afraid Andy will tell them the whole thing and then I honestly don't know *what* will happen.

Patricia is watching me as I write this. She is in her bed across the room. Next door, I can hear Andy pacing the floor.

Wednesday, September 3

At breakfast this morning Andy told Patricia and me that we're all going to a party together this Saturday night. He said it's a birthday party for his friend Paul Gaddis, and he said there'd be a lot of nice people there and we'd all have a good time. I told him I wasn't sure I'd be able to make it, and Patricia asked me did I have a date for this Saturday, and I said No, but there was a movie I'd planned on seeing, and they both said I could go see the movie any time at all, but this was a birthday party, and Andy had gone to a lot of trouble to get us invited to it. So I was trapped into saying I'd go.

When I told Jack about this at work, he said I was a fool. He said I should break off with Andy as soon as possible, let him know it's finished between us, and not go with him to parties or *any*place. I promised I'd tell Andy tonight.

Well, we just got back from a long walk, and I *tried* to tell him, but he just wouldn't listen. He just wouldn't understand. To begin with, Patricia wanted to come along with us when we said we were going for a walk, but Andy said he wanted to discuss some of the courses he was thinking about registering for—registration is Monday—and since I was the one who'd looked through the catalog with him, he thought it'd be better if we talked it over alone. He didn't want to talk at *all*, of course. What he wanted to do was what he always wanted to do. He started walking me over toward his car, and he asked me if I'd like to take a ride out to the beach, and I said No, I had to go to work the next morning, it'd take us at least an hour to get out to Sands Spit, and he said he had the beach over at Henley Island in mind, be a nice night to just sit there on the beach and look out at the ocean. I told him I didn't feel like going out to the beach, and he said Well, let's get in the car anyway, okay, Mure? I said No, I didn't want to get in the car because I knew what he had in mind, and I wasn't in the mood for anything like that tonight. In fact, there were some things we had to talk about, some very serious things.

He changed the subject right then and there, told me how much he was looking forward to starting school next week, and how right I was about waiting before we got married, dispensation might take a while anyway, if ever we applied for it, though we didn't have to, we could just get married at City Hall, the way he'd suggested earlier. I tried to break in at that point, tried to tell him I didn't want to get married at *all*, but he changed that around, too, made it sound as if I was agreeing it would be a good thing to wait a little while. I tried three or four times to get him to understand that I wanted to break off with him, that I honestly didn't love him anymore, but he just wouldn't listen, and I never could get past the first couple of words before he jumped in with something to change the subject. It was impossible.

We got home about fifteen minutes ago, and he's in the living room watching television right this minute. Patricia's in there, too. I've *got* to tell him. Jack will be furious with me when he learns I didn't tell him. But if Andy won't listen, what am I supposed to do?

Thursday, September 4

Tonight I told him.

I got very frightened at one point.

But I told him. And it's over with. I think it's over with.

After supper Aunt Lillian asked Uncle Frank if he'd take her out shopping. This is Thursday night, and all the department stores are open till nine. So he said okay, and they went out and left Patricia and me to do the dishes. Patricia had to go to the library, to get a book she needed for a class assignment, so she left at about seven-thirty, and Andy and I were all alone in the house. He had gone to his room right after supper, and he was in there with the door closed. I was really afraid to knock on his door, so I went into the living room for a while and watched television, but I knew I had to do it sooner or later, I was just building my courage. At about a quarter to eight I went across the hall and knocked on his door, and he told me to come in. He was lying on his bed with his hands behind his head. He was wearing only his undershorts. I said I wanted to talk to him and he said Sure, what about? I told him I wanted to talk about us, and then I closed the door and went to sit in a wingback chair he had across from the bed in his room. I was still wearing the dress I'd worn to work that day, I hadn't changed when I got home. The dress and a ribbon in my hair and pantyhose and the blue shoes with the French heels. The television was on in the living room, I could hear a telephone ringing on it, and then the squeal of an automobile's tires, doors opening and closing, voices.

Well, what is it? Andy said, and I told him we had to end this thing that was going on between us. I told him it had begun to bother me last month, when I thought I was pregnant, and when I realized how wrong it would be to bring a child into the world whose parents were blood relatives. I told him I was still very fond of him, but that what we'd been doing was wrong, and I couldn't go on doing it, not feeling the way I did now. I told him that there were plenty of men and women in the world without cousins having to start up with each other.

He said *You* started it, Muriel.

I said Well, I don't really know *who* started it, Andy, I just know I fell in love with you back there in April, and what happened was just something neither one of us could control, I guess. All I'm saying now is that I really want to end it, and I hope you'll just permit it to die, Andy.

It must've been a quarter past eight by then, I've shortened it a lot, but it must've taken me at *least* a half-hour to get it all out. During that time the television was going outside, it almost sounded as if there were people in the house besides us, people with their own problems and their own lives, thrashing them out on television the way we were thrashing them out there in Andy's room. After I told him, he just lay there on his bed for the longest time without saying anything at all, so finally I got up to go, and he said Sit down, Muriel. And then it all came out. He told me how much he loved me, told me he'd tried so hard to stay away from me in the beginning, realizing we were cousins and knowing it was wrong. But then, when he saw I was interested, he figured he could dare to make a move, I'd been living there in the house for more than two years by then, he'd never so much as touched my hand in all that time, but now he felt he could dare, because he saw I was interested at last. And even then, even after it was plain to both of us what was eventually going to happen, even then he'd tried to stop it, knowing all along he was lost. And so now he was really lost, now I was abandoning him—was that it?

No I said, I'm merely trying to tell you that we've got to stop, Andy.

Stop what? he said. Stop *loving* you? How can I do that? Do you want me to kill myself, Muriel? Do you want me to die? I'll die without you, you know.

You won't die, I said.

Take off your dress, he said.

He said it so suddenly, he still wasn't looking at me, he still had his hands behind his head, he was still staring up at the ceiling.

Take off your dress, he said.

I asked him why he wanted me to take off my dress, and he said I *knew* why, just take the damn thing off. You've been driving me crazy for the past God knows how long, he said, just take off your fucking dress, he said, you owe me at least one more time.

I told him I didn't owe him anything, and that was when he got off the bed, swung his legs off the side of the bed, and came toward me and said Take off the dress, Muriel, I'm not kidding. I was frightened by then, I was really frightened. There was a crazy look on his face, I was afraid he was going to hit me. He grabbed my wrist and forced me down on my knees, but I wouldn't take off the dress, I wouldn't help him. I told him he had better not hurt me, and he said he wasn't going to hurt me, but I was going to do what he wanted me to do, and then he said Go on, take it, I know you want it, and I did what he told me to do because I really was afraid he would hurt me. Afterwards, he went to the bed and lay face down on it and began crying. I really felt very sorry for him, I almost reached out to touch his hair with my hand. There was only the sound of his crying and the television set going outside, a doorbell ringing, and then I realized it wasn't the television set at all, it was the *real* doorbell, it was the *apartment* doorbell. So I went out of Andy's room, closing the door behind me, and I went to the front door and opened it.

It was Patricia. She had forgotten her key, she said.

I told her to come in.

She asked me if everything was all right. She was looking at me peculiarly.

I told her everything was all right.

I hope to God it is.

Friday, September 5

Someone has read this diary.

The strap was cut when I took it out of the drawer tonight, so I know someone has read it. I'm sure it was Andy. I remember a while ago when he asked me was I writing about us in the diary, and I told him I was. I think he wanted to see what I've been writing. It frightens me to think that he read all the stuff I wrote about Jack. I don't know what's going on inside his head. I think he's still very angry, and feels he hasn't yet got back at me. Even after last night, even after what he made me do last night. I'm not sure he thinks he's even with me. At least not yet. It's so strange. I loved him so much, and now I only feel afraid of him, and a little sorry for him. And he loved me, too, or at least he claims he did, and now he feels nothing but hate—I can see it burning in his eyes.

At supper tonight he said he wouldn't be coming to the party tomorrow. He said the restaurant had called and asked him to work tomorrow night, and he'd told them he would. I'm sure he doesn't *have* to go to work tomorrow night if he doesn't want to. He just can't stand being anywhere near me, that's all. He can't stand the sight of me now that I've ended it. So Patricia and I will have go to the party alone, an idea Aunt Lillian doesn't like, two girls coming home late at night from a party. Patricia calmed her somewhat by telling her we'd be home by eleven sharp, but Aunt Lillian *still* doesn't like the idea. *I* don't want to go to the stupid thing at all. All I want to do now is move ahead with my own life, get out of this place as soon as possible, find an apartment of my own, see what happens between Jack and me.

At lunch today I told him all about last night, my finally telling Andy we were through, and how he'd practically raped me. Jack said he'd be very happy when I got out of that house once and for all. And then he said something that got me very fluttery all over again. He said And once *you're* out, Mure, we'll see about *my* getting out. I knew he was talking about his wife. I knew he was talking about leaving her.

So tomorrow night I'll go to a dull party I don't *want* to go to, and then I'll only have Sunday to get through till I can see Jack again on Monday.

But at least the worst is over with.

I've ended it with Andy, and I can breathe again.

Ten

Patricia Lowery's grandmother recognized Carella from his earlier visit, but this time he was accompanied by a tall blond man he introduced as his partner, Detective Kling. She said she would have to check with her granddaughter before she let them in the apartment, and then closed and locked the door, leaving them to cool their heels in the hallway for a while. Kling had not yet read the diary. Carella had briefed him on it, however, and had also voiced the regret that he could not charge Jack Armstrong, All-American Boy, with any crime but Attempted Seduction of the Innocent—which could not be found in the state's Penal Law, and which in fact was only a violation of Carella's own moral code, a Class E misdemeanor at best. Old Grandma Lowery was a spry old lady, but it took her ten minutes to get back to the front door with word that her granddaughter would most certainly talk to the detectives. They followed her through the apartment into the back bedroom, where Patricia sat in an armchair with a book open on her lap. There was no place else to sit, except the bed, so both detectives remained standing while they talked to her.

"Patricia," Carella said, "I've just finished reading Muriel's diary, and I'd like to ask you a few questions about it."

"Sure," Patricia said, and nodded.

"To begin with, have *you* read that diary?"

"No," Patricia said.

"You're sure about that?"

"How could I have read it? She kept it locked."

"Well, you could have cut the strap, for example," Carella said.

"Why would I do that?"

"You might have done that if you were curious about what was in the diary."

"I didn't care about what was in the diary," Patricia said.

"But you once asked Muriel what she found to write about, didn't you?"

"I don't remember."

"Yes, that was on . . . let me see," Carella said, and consulted his notes, and said, "That was on Wednesday, August twenty-seventh. You asked Muriel what she could possibly find to write about each night. Do you remember that?"

"I really don't. But if that's what Muriel wrote in her diary . . ."

"Yes, that's what she wrote."

"Then I suppose it's true."

"Well, I think we've got to assume that *everything* in the diary is true, don't you think?"

"Yes, I never knew Muriel to lie about anything."

"And she certainly wouldn't have lied to the diary, because there'd have been no reason for it. So we've got to assume, for example, that when she says her boss's name is Jack Armstrong, why that's her boss's name. Am I right?"

"Yes," Patricia said, and nodded.

"You've never met him, though."

"No, never."

"And when she says in the diary that Jack Armstrong has brown hair and blue eyes, why, then we've got to believe it."

"Yes."

"You wouldn't know whether that's true or not, Patricia, because you've never met the man. But if

Muriel said it was so, why, then I guess we have to believe it. Anyway, I *have* met the man, and he *does* have brown hair and blue eyes, so we know she was telling the truth at least in that instance."

"Mm-huh," Patricia said.

"And I guess we've got to assume she was telling the truth about everything else as well," Carella said.

This time Patricia only nodded. She was watching Carella intently, not seeming to understand what he was getting at, studying his face for clues. Kling looked a little baffled, too.

"Patricia, when I spoke to you yesterday," Carella said, "you told me that the last time you saw Muriel's diary was on September fifth, the night before she was murdered."

"That's right," Patricia said.

"You said you saw her writing in it."

"Yes. She was sitting at the desk writing in it."

"And where were you?"

"In bed."

"And when she finished writing in it, what did she do?"

"She locked it and put it back in her drawer."

"She carried the key on a chain around her neck, isn't that what you told me?"

"Yes."

"Could you see her clearly when she was locking the diary? I mean, was there plenty of light in the room, and was she standing close enough for you to see what she was doing?"

"She was sitting, actually. At the desk."

"But you could see her clearly."

"Yes."

"Patricia, I'm going to tell you about some things that are bothering me," Carella said. "I'm going to be completely honest with you, and I hope you'll be completely honest in return. Okay?"

"I've been honest with you all along," Patricia said.

"Well, that's not quite true, is it? You lied to us that first time we talked to you, didn't you? You said the murderer was a man with dark hair and blue eyes . . ."

"Well, yes, but I told you the truth later."

"In fact, that's one of the things that's bothering me, Patricia. That business about describing the murderer the way you first did. Because, you see, in Muriel's diary, it's pretty plain to see that Jack Armstrong is interested in her, and here's someone forcing Muriel to commit a sex act, and you describe . . ."

"He *did* force her to do it."

"Yes. And he looked like Jack Armstrong, according to your first description. Except that you'd never *met* Jack Armstrong, of course, and you couldn't have known what he looked like. Unless you'd read Muriel's diary."

"No, I didn't read Muriel's diary."

"I know. You just told me that a few minutes ago, and you also said you'd be honest with me. But I think we've agreed that Muriel told the truth in her diary, am I right?"

"Yes."

"Then I must tell you that on September fourth, Muriel wrote about someone asking her to take off her dress and forcing her to commit a sex act against her will. She wrote that on September fourth. It was everything you described as having taken place on September sixth—two days later. *Except* the murder, of course. But everything else was there in the diary, just as you later described it. Now how do you account for that, Patricia?"

"I don't know what you mean," Patricia said.

"Patricia, you *did* read Muriel's diary, didn't you?"

"No."

"Patricia, the strap on the diary was cut, someone read that diary."

"Then it was Andy. If anyone read it, it had to be Andy."

"Patricia, it was you."

"I'm telling you I did *not* . . ."

"Because the September fifth entry started with the words '*Someone has read this diary. The strap was cut when I took it out of the drawer tonight.'* This is in my notes, Patricia, it's a direct quote from your cousin's diary."

"So what? I still don't understand . . ."

"Not five minutes ago you told me you saw your cousin *lock* the diary after she finished writing in it that night, the night of September fifth, the night before she was killed. Now, Patricia, if the strap had already been cut, why on earth would your cousin have locked . . . ?"

The scream came unexpectedly.

She did not rise from the chair. She simply threw back her head, and the scream erupted from her mouth, and her eyes above the scream were wide with horror. The scream seemed eternal. It chilled both detectives to the marrow.

When it ended, they put handcuffs on her wrists.

She was only fifteen years old, and so they questioned her in the office of Peter Hudd, the lawyer appointed to defend her, rather than in the police station. Fifteen-year-olds weren't supposed to be interrogated in police stations. Most police officers interrogated them there anyway—usually in the locker room or the swing room or someplace that didn't *seem* like part of a police station, though actually it was. The upper age limit for a juvenile offender in this state was sixteen years old, and the code stated that a delinquent was a child who violated any law or any municipal ordinance or who committed any act which, if committed by an adult, would be a serious crime, *except* (and this was where Patricia Lowery's luck ran out) any child *fifteen* years of age who committed any act which, if committed by an adult, would be a crime punishable by death or life imprisonment. Patricia Lowery had allegedly committed a crime punishable by life imprisonment.

She had told them two versions of the same murderous tale, and now she told them the third and final version, and this one they accepted as the truth, even though there had been some truth in the previous two versions as well. It was this final truth, however, that could set her brother free and send Patricia to jail for life. They listened attentively. The stenographer took down every word. Carella conducted the interrogation. Patricia's voice was barely audible. She sat shivering throughout, hugging herself with both arms.

CARELLA: Do you want to tell us what happened?
PATRICIA: I've already *told* you what happened.
CARELLA: But you weren't telling the truth.
PATRICIA: That was only the first time. I told you the truth later. Don't you remember? I came to the station house and I told you the truth.
CARELLA: You came to the station house the first time, too.
PATRICIA: Yes, but . . .
CARELLA: And you lied.
PATRICIA: Yes, but *not* the second time. I told you the truth that time. My brother killed her.
CARELLA: Patricia, you said you would talk to us. Your lawyer here has no objection to your telling us the truth, so why don't you tell us what really happened?
PATRICIA: I just hate to have to go over this again and again and again. You took it all down the first time, and then I said it on tape the second time, now you want it again. I mean, how many times do I have to tell you the same damn *thing*?
CARELLA: Just this last time, and that'll be it.
PATRICIA: It's freezing in here. Can't someone turn up the heat a little?
CARELLA: Mr. Hudd?
HUDD: I'll get it.
CARELLA: Patricia, why don't you just start from the beginning?
PATRICIA: The party, do you mean?
CARELLA: Wherever the beginning was.
PATRICIA: Well, that *was* the beginning.

CARELLA: Okay, what happened?

PATRICIA: I took the knife.

CARELLA: Why?

PATRICIA: Because Muriel and I had to walk home alone, why do you think? So I spied the knife on the kitchen rack and I just slipped it into my bag.

CARELLA: Then what?

PATRICIA: Then we started walking home.

CARELLA: What time was that?

PATRICIA: I *told* you all this already, I don't know why I have to tell you again.

CARELLA: This is the first time you told us about the knife.

PATRICIA: You just don't listen.

CARELLA: You took the knife from the rack. Where was the rack?

PATRICIA: In the kitchen. Paul Gaddis's kitchen. That's where the knife was. In the kitchen. I heard them when I came in.

CARELLA: Heard who?

PATRICIA: I went in the kitchen, you see, to get myself a glass of milk, and that's when I heard them.

CARELLA: I don't understand.

PATRICIA: Because you don't listen.

CARELLA: I'm listening, but I don't understand who you mean. You say you heard them— *Who* did you hear?

PATRICIA: Muriel and Andy.

CARELLA: In Paul Gaddis's kitchen?

PATRICIA: No, no. In the bedroom.

CARELLA: Patricia . . .

PATRICIA: They were in Andy's bedroom, what's so difficult to understand about that?

CARELLA: What were they doing in the bedroom, Patricia?

PATRICIA: How should I know? Ask my darling brother what they were doing. Ask Muriel.

CARELLA: Muriel is dead, Patricia.

PATRICIA: Don't I know it? He killed her.

CARELLA: Who did?

PATRICIA: My brother. Stuck it into her. I told her, don't think I didn't tell her. When it started raining so hard, and we ran to the building, and the ceiling looked pregnant, the ceiling overhead where we were standing, it was ugly and bloated, it looked pregnant. I said to her, I had the knife in my handbag, you see, so I wasn't afraid anybody would attack us or anything, I was quite calm in the hallway there, I said to her she must have been terribly frightened that time, and she asked me what time did I mean and I said Why, when you thought you were pregnant, Muriel. There was light shining from the streetlamp, I could see her very clearly, the rain was falling so hard, so hard, she looked at me, and I could see the surprise on her face, and she said You read my diary, didn't you, you're the one who read my diary, and I said Yes, Muriel, I'm the one who read your diary, and she said Why'd you do that, Patricia? I'm freezing to death here, aren't there any blankets in here?

CARELLA: Could someone get her a blanket, please? Go ahead, Patricia.

PATRICIA: *Freeze* to death in here.

CARELLA: What'd you say when she asked you why you'd read the diary?

PATRICIA: Oh, what *could* I say, use your head. Could I tell her I knew all about her and my darling brother, knew from when I'd come home from the library and heard them in the bedroom, you can hear *every*thing in that house. They didn't know I was home, the television was on, I guess the noise of the television drowned out my coming in —but it didn't drown out what they were doing in that bedroom, oh no. Forcing her to get on her knees, and telling her to take it, and her *doing* it, God, the *noises* she made! I hated her from that minute, I wanted to kill her right then, I *would* have killed her if I had the nerve. But I was afraid he'd turn on *me*, you see, I was afraid he'd force *me* to do the same thing, because . . . well . . . he's always loved me, you see, I know he loves me more than Muriel, so he probably *would* have forced me to do the same thing. So I ran outside again, and then I rang the doorbell and pretended I'd forgotten my key— *Is* someone getting a blanket?

CARELLA: Yes, Patricia.

PATRICIA: Because it really *is* freezing in here, you know.

CARELLA: She wanted to know why you'd read the diary . . .

PATRICIA: Yes, and I told her I'd read it because I'd heard them in Andy's room, and I couldn't believe what I'd heard, so I read the diary to find out if it was true, and it *was* true. Do you deny it? I said. Do you deny it? And she said No, I don't deny it, and that was when I took the knife out of my bag and stabbed her. I don't know how many times I stabbed her. I finally ripped her pantyhose around the crotch and stuck the knife inside her. Then I just stood there in the hall, she was lying on the floor, I said Muriel, what's the matter with you? and I realized she was dead, I knew I had killed her. So I ripped my own dress with the knife, and cut the palms of my hands to make it seem somebody had tried to kill *me*, too, and I cut my own cheek, and then I ran out of the building and threw the knife down the sewer and went to the station house.

CARELLA: Why did you describe the killer as a man with dark hair and blue eyes?

PATRICIA: I don't know. I guess it was . . . well, I really don't know. I guess because of what I read in the diary. About what was happening with her and the man at the bank. I guess I got confused there. I guess . . . I guess I figured she'd do the same thing with him that she'd already done with Andy, yes, maybe that was it. She probably *would* have done the same thing, don't you think? If somebody hadn't killed her? Don't you think?

CARELLA: Why did you later tell us . . . ?

PATRICIA: Don't you think?

CARELLA: I really don't know, Patricia.

PATRICIA: Oh, yes. It was in her diary. She said so herself. She said she felt like a wild animal.

CARELLA: Patricia, you came to us later and said your brother had killed her. Why did you do that?

PATRICIA: Because, you see, I didn't think he was . . . you see, I thought *she* was the one who'd . . . who'd *done* all this, throwing herself at him, you know. And I thought if I killed her, well, if *somebody* killed her, why, then she'd be punished for what she'd done, and my brother wouldn't have to bother with her any more, everything would be all right again. Because, you see, I *knew* he loved me more than he loved her, no matter *what* I heard him saying that day in his room, and no matter what she wrote in her diary. I mean, I'm his *sister*, he's got to love his sister more than he does his cousin, isn't that right? He's just *got* to.

CARELLA: What made you change your mind?

PATRICIA: I changed my mind, that's right.

CARELLA: Yes, you accused him of murdering her. You said he'd killed her.

PATRICIA: Yes.

CARELLA: Why?
PATRICIA: Because he jumped on the coffin. He said he loved her.

Immediately following the interrogation, Patricia Lowery's attorney asked that she be moved to the psychiatric ward of Buena Vista Hospital for observation pending arraignment. He and the assistant district attorney batted around the technicalities of this for several minutes, and it was finally agreed that justice could as easily be served in a locked cell at the hospital as in one of the holding cells in the basement of the 87th Precinct. The ambulance arrived some ten minutes after they phoned for it. Carella took the handcuffs from Patricia's wrists, and one of the ambulance attendants helped her into a strait jacket, and then signed a release stating he had taken the prisoner into custody. The attendants led her out of the office then, and down the corridor to the elevator. Attorney Hudd asked if anyone would care for a drink, and the detectives and the assistant district attorney declined, and Hudd said he guessed it was time to close shop for the night. He checked out the burglar-alarm system, activated it, and then stepped quickly into the corridor in the thirty seconds of delay-time allotted to him. On the sidewalk outside, he said goodnight to the other men and began walking toward the garage where he customarily parked his car.

"Nuttier'n a fruitcake, that girl," the assistant D.A. said. "Wouldn't be surprised if that's why Hudd agreed to let her talk. Anybody reading that transcript'll know in a minute she's crazy."

Carella said nothing.

"Probably won't even get to stand trial, she's that far gone. All your work down the drain," he said. He shook hands with both detectives then, and started off up the street.

"Think I'll walk over to Augusta's," Kling said.

"Okay," Carella said. "See you in the morning, huh?"

"Yeah," Kling said.

Carella watched as he walked off. He turned then, and began walking in the opposite direction, toward the subway kiosk two blocks away. As he walked he kept thinking of the moment Patricia Lowery had thrown back her head and begun screaming.

It started raining just as he went down the steps into the subway.

ABOUT THE AUTHOR

ED MCBAIN is actually famed novelist Evan Hunter, but millions know him as Ed McBain, top cop writer in the world and author of the 87th Precinct series. Praised by *The New York Times* as "the best of today's procedural school of police stories," the series now has well over 53,000,000 copies in print around the world. McBain has been writing the 87th Precinct thrillers for the past twenty-four years. Fans can count on the realism of police activities in the series; the details are authentic and have become a McBain trademark.

Ed McBain (or Evan Hunter) grew up on the tough city streets of New York with one main ambition: to get out. At first he thought his ticket would be his artistic skills, but during a two-year stint in the Navy, he discovered a new talent: writing short stories. After attending Hunter College, he spent a disastrous few months teaching high school. Hunter turned that experience into a sizzling novel, later made into a film, called *Blackboard Jungle*. He's been writing steadily ever since, not only the 87th Precinct series, but such novels as *Strangers When We Meet, Last Summer,* and the script for Hitchcock's celebrated horror film, *The Birds*. Evan Hunter and his wife, Mary Vann, divide their time between Connecticut and Sarasota, Florida.